D0611851

Please Return To:
Grace Christian School Library
325 M-140
Watervliet, MI 49098
616-463-5545

Crossway Books for Young People by Stephen Bly

THE NATHAN T. RIGGINS WESTERN ADVENTURE SERIES

The Dog Who Would Not Smile
Coyote True
You Can Always Trust a Spotted Horse
The Last Stubborn Buffalo in Nevada
Never Dance with a Bobcat
Hawks Don't Say Goodbye

THE LEWIS AND CLARK SQUAD ADVENTURE SERIES

Intrigue at the Rafter B Ranch
The Secret of the Old Rifle
Treachery at the River Canyon
Revenge on Eagle Island
Danger at Deception Pass
Hazards of the Half-Court Press

RETTA BARRE'S OREGON TRAIL

The Lost Wagon Train
The Buffalo's Last Stand
The Plain Prairie Princess

ADVENTURES ON THE AMERICAN FRONTIER

Daring Rescue at Sonora Pass
Dangerous Ride Across Humboldt Flats
Mysterious Robbery on the Utah Plains

Adventures on the American Frontier ★ Book 1

Daring Rescue at Sonora Pass

Stephen Bly

CROSSWAY BOOKS
A DIVISION OF
GOOD NEWS PUBLISHERS
WHEATON, ILLINOIS

Daring Rescue at Sonora Pass

Published by Crossway Books
a division of Good News Publishers
1300 Crescent Street
Wheaton, Illinois 60187

Cover design: David LaPlaca

Cover illustration: Vito DiAngi

First printing, 2003

Printed in the United States of America

Library of Congress Cataloging-in-Publication Data

Bly, Stephen A., 1944 -
Daring rescue at Sonora Pass / Stephen Bly.
p. cm. — (Adventures on the American Frontier ; bk. 1)
Summary: The Joyton family, who run the Sonora Pass stagecoach station, deal with the mysterious shooting death of a passenger and welcome new neighbors who open a mercantile next door.
ISBN 1-58134-471-6 (TPB)
[1. Stagecoach stations—Fiction. 2. Frontier and pioneer life—Arizona—Fiction. 3. General stores—Fiction. 4. Robbers and outlaws—Fiction. 5. Arizona—History—To 1912—Fiction.] I. Title. II. Series.
PZ7.B6275Dar 2003
[Fic]—dc22 2003009872

DP 13 12 11 10 09 08 07 06 05 04 03
15 14 13 12 11 10 9 8 7 6 5 4 3 2 1

"And who knoweth
whether thou art
come to the kingdom
for such a time as this?"

ESTHER 4:14 (KJV)

Author's Note

The first regular stagecoach route to the California goldfields was a good thousand miles longer than it needed to be. John Butterfield built the Oxbow Route from Memphis and St. Louis to please certain southern politicians. They insisted on a route through nearly unoccupied lands in west Texas, New Mexico, and Arizona. The 2,800-mile trip was calculated to take twenty-five days (576½ hours to be exact). Posted at every stage stop and station were these words from Butterfield: "Every person in the Company's employ will remember that each minute is of importance. If each driver on the route loses fifteen minutes, it would make a total loss of time on the entire route of twenty-five hours, or more than one day."

Large deluxe Concord wagons were used on the smooth roads. Tough Celerity wagons were used on the rough roads. Both provided a jarring, dusty, usually monotonous ride. No extra time was allowed for ferries, changing teams, or letting the passengers off to eat. The drivers were supposed to gain time for such activities. The average speed was four and a half miles per hour. For any man to leave civilization behind and staff a stagecoach station in the territory of the Chiricahua Apache was an act of unusual bravery. To move a whole family to such a location demonstrated legendary faith and courage.

The Joytons are one such family. In the isolated desert they discover natural beauty, family intimacy, and daily trust in God's provision. Some will feel sorry for them. Others will envy them.

Stagecoaches have fascinated me since the second to the last station on that fabled Oxbow Route was Visalia, California, the place of my birth.

Stephen Bly
Winchester, Idaho
Spring of 2003

ONE

Friday, June 1, 1859, Sonora Pass Station, Arizona Territory

Talby Joyton hurdled the low adobe wall and waved a brass telescope above his head. "They just passed Scalp Creek, and Whap Martin is holdin' the ribbons."

"How many on top?" Mrs. Joyton called from the front step of the station.

"Two others besides Whap and J. J.," Talby shouted.

Ceva Joyton spun around and ducked as she entered the five-foot, five-inch doorway. "Blaze, set the table for twelve with two spares in the kitchen."

Drew Joyton, fourteen, led two black horses to his father at the rail. "Daddy, Whap is drivin'. We've got time. He never wants to hurry Mama's cookin'."

Rand Joyton harnessed the two horses. His years of practice made it look as easy as leashing a cocker spaniel. "It don't matter, son. We hook them up as fast as we can. No driver has ever had to wait at Sonora Pass. That's our reputation."

Talby raced over to his brother and father. "You reckon they have my balsa wood?"

"I told you it would take two months to get that balsa here from New York City. Maybe longer," Drew said.

"I don't know why it should take so long. I could ride the stagecoach to St. Louis, take a train to New York and buy it, and come back here quicker than that."

Mr. Joyton laughed. "I reckon you could, son."

Talby ran to the ladder that leaned against the house. "You want me to go on the roof and signal you?"

"That would be fine since you're goin' to do it whether I say so or not," Mr. Joyton replied.

Drew brought another pair of gray horses out of the corral.

"They just passed Deception Rock!" Talby shouted down from his perch next to the granite river-rock chimney on top of the cedar-shake roof.

Mrs. Joyton stooped through the doorway. "Do you see any women in the coach?" she called to her son on the roof. A red hen led her chicks across the packed-dirt yard.

"I can't see anyone in the coach. They must be leanin' back and sleepin'," Talby shouted.

"No one sleeps coming up the Sonora Pass grade with Whap Martin driving," Mrs. Joyton remarked. "Drew, when you're through helping Daddy, draw me up another bucket of well water—only strain out the bugs this time."

Blaze Joyton stooped under the short doorframe and stood on the front porch. "Everything is all set, Mama."

"Thanks, honey. You pour the coffee as soon as Whap stops the wagon."

Drew brought the final pair of horses out to his father. As he stood waiting, he gazed at his mother and sister. "Joyton women are quite handsome, Daddy. Did you ever notice that?"

Rand Joyton glanced over at the ladies. "I think I might have noticed it a time or two."

"Maybe they're the purdiest redheaded mama and daughter in the territory," Drew added.

"I know they're the tallest mama and daughter pair in the territory." Mr. Joyton continued to harness the horses.

"I think I'm as tall as Mama. You need to measure me again."

"Drew, you'll be taller than me within the year," Mr. Joyton said. "I've got this crew about lashed down. You go stand ready for that six-up that Whap is bringin' us."

"They're at Washburn Creek, and Whap ain't slowin' them one tad," Talby shouted down.

"Whap always drives like he was tryin' to impress Mr. Butterfield himself," Mr. Joyton said. "He must have gotten behind schedule back down the line."

Drew stationed himself along the road next to the low adobe wall. He surveyed the grounds. To the south stretched the treeless, smooth-topped Dragoon Mountains. In the foreground, large granite boulders the size of privies outlined the yard. Three green-leafed cottonwoods circled the well. The adobe-fenced corrals checkered up against the base of Frenchman's Mountain. The tall adobe barn had the look of a Spanish Mission from the distance and had fooled more than one pilgrim.

The station house sprawled room by room across the mountain pass, surrounded by a three-foot adobe wall and a packed-dirt yard that housed six to twelve chickens, depending on the shade. To the north, the mountain dropped off like a giant slide. Drew could see across the valley for a hundred empty miles.

Mr. Joyton, six-up team in hand, waited at the corrals.

Mrs. Joyton stood with arms crossed over her green gingham dress and white apron at the gateless opening to the road.

Sixteen-year-old Blaze, wearing her hair in a long auburn braid, stood without hat or bonnet at the front step, her hands folded at her waist.

The shortest of the Joytons, twelve-year-old Talby, was still scouting from the shake roof of the station.

Drew heard the thunder of twenty-four hooves.

The squeak of dry axles.

And watched the fog of yellow-brown dirt race ahead of the stagecoach.

Whap Martin hollered, yanked the lead lines, and stomped on the hand brake. The huge Concord stagecoach slid to a stop between Drew and his mother. J. J. Jones shoved his shotgun under the coach seat and climbed down.

"Afternoon, Mrs. Joyton," Whap hollered as if the hooves were still pounding.

"Welcome to Sonora Pass, all of you. How many for dinner, Mr. Martin?" she called out as Drew unhitched the team.

"Only us four," Martin replied as he hopped down.

Ceva Joyton glanced back at the coach. "Only four? You mean, there's no one in the coach?"

"No one except a dead man," J. J. Jones told her. "I don't reckon he'll be eatin'."

"Oh, dear," Mrs. Joyton said. "Did you have Apache trouble again?"

A well-dressed man in a gray suit and gray hat covered with yellow-brown dust climbed off the stage behind Jones. "Not hardly, ma'am. He shot himself."

A small, unshaven man with nervous, dark eyes also climbed down. His suit coat was patched at the elbows, his white shirt yellowed at the collar. "He yanked his pocket pistol out and accidentally shot himself in the heart. I ain't never seen anything like it."

Drew tried to hear the conversation as he led the six-horse team away from the wagon. But by the time he pulled the rigging and turned the horses out, everyone had gone into the station dining room except his father.

"What's this about a man shooting himself, Daddy?"

Mr. Joyton continued to hook up the fresh horses to the stagecoach. "Take a peek for yourself."

Drew shoved his black boot on the step and raised himself up. A man in a black frockcoat lay slumped over the rear seat. "Did he really shoot himself?"

"That's what the two passengers said."

"Why was he pulling his gun?"

"That's what they don't know. They thought he was reaching for a cigar. Suddenly there was an explosion."

"What're we goin' to do?"

"Hook up this team and go eat dinner. There isn't much you can do for a dead man. You go on. Tell Mama I'll be right in."

Drew leaned down to enter the dining room. Big windows on the north side made the room bright without any lanterns. The two drivers and two passengers sat at the east end of the long table set for twelve. Talby sat at the other end.

Mrs. Joyton and Blaze served the food in large, bright-colored pottery bowls.

"Is your daddy comin' in?" Whap Martin mumbled through a big bite of brown gravy and stew.

The multicolored hooked rug muted Drew's steps. "Yes, sir. He'll be right in."

The stage driver waved his knife at Drew and his brother and then at Blaze and Mrs. Joyton. "Did you boys ever see a family as tall as the Joytons? Makes me and J. J. seem like dwarves ever' time we stop. Must be the spring water here at Sonora Pass."

Drew plopped down next to his brother. "Talby, did you see that dead guy?" he whispered.

"No. Mama wouldn't let me look," Talby whispered back. "Did you see him?"

"Yeah."

"How did he look?"

"Dead." Drew shrugged.

"Was there blood and guts ever'where?"

"He was slumped over. I couldn't see anything."

"Was his eyes open?"

"Couldn't tell."

"You didn't see very much," Talby muttered.

Blaze set out bowls of apple cobbler and then sat on the bench next to Drew. He handed her the bowl of stew.

"I'm not very hungry," she said. "I can't believe we're all in here eating, and there's a dead man in the stage."

"What're we supposed to do?" Drew asked.

"At least someone could pull a blanket over him."

"He ain't cold," Talby remarked.

"That's not the point," Blaze insisted.

Drew sopped his bread in the brown gravy. "Maybe everyone is trying to figure out what to do next."

Blaze raised her thick, sweeping red eyebrows.

"Eh, why don't I go cover him up with a blanket?" Drew offered.

His sister nodded and took a helping of stew.

When Drew returned, his father had just entered the dining room. "There's room at the big table today, Daddy," Blaze called out. "Mama said we could eat in here."

He jammed his hat on a peg in the wall. "I'll be there after I wash up, darlin'."

"Say, Rand, I need to talk with you," Whap Martin called out.

Mr. Joyton washed his hands in an enameled tin basin near the front doorway and then grabbed a half-clean towel. "What's that, Whap?"

Martin wiped his mouth on the back of his hand. "Can you bury that ol' boy here at Sonora Pass?"

"Bury him?" Rand rubbed the back of his neck. "We don't have a cemetery."

Whap dumped more salt on his stew. "Don't need to be nothin' formal. Just wrap him in a blanket and shove him in a hole. It ain't permanent."

"Mr. Martin," Ceva Joyton interrupted as she brought in a fresh loaf of sourdough bread, "that hardly seems the Christian thing to do. No person should be hurriedly tossed in a hole. Each life is precious in God's sight."

Martin tore off a quarter of the loaf of bread and painted it thick with butter. "Yes, ma'am. It surely is. But this old boy bought a ticket clear to Visalia, California. His body would be decomposed if we took him the whole way. So he has to be put down someplace until his family can claim him."

"Couldn't you take him to Tucson?" she asked. "They have undertakers and cemeteries there."

Blaze scurried out to the kitchen.

"Maybe in the winter he would last," J. J. said with a big spoon of cobbler only inches from his mouth. "But not in the June heat. Besides, there are other folks between here and Tucson that are countin' on takin' the stage west. They ain't goin' to share a bench with a dead man."

Ceva glanced at her husband.

Rand Joyton picked his teeth with his fingernail and rammed in another bite of gravy-covered meat. "I reckon Whap is right. We'll bury him here until his kin come to claim him."

Blaze made the rounds refilling coffee cups.

Whap took a gulp and swallowed it hot. "Thank you, folks," he wheezed. "I might need to borrow a little soda and hot water to clean up my coach."

"If there is blood, use cold water," Ceva instructed.

Martin and Jones topped off another bowl of stew, ate two helpings of pie, refilled canteens, unloaded the body, and cleaned the coach while the two passengers finished dinner.

Drew squatted next to the dead man. *Lord, people don't look human when they're dead. He's like a carving. A soft statue. Well, not too soft. It's our spirit that makes us who we are, isn't it? When you take that away, we got no more personality than a rock.*

The man with the gray hat stepped over next to him. Drew covered the body back up with the wool blanket and stood.

"You studyin' the man?" he asked Drew.

"I guess I was talkin' to the Lord about him."

"That's good, son. What in the world is a nice Christian family doin' way out in this wilderness?"

"Mama's chest don't hurt, and she doesn't cough blood so much up here."

"Don't the Indians harass you?"

"We have a little trouble now and then. But the army has been patrolling it pretty good."

"What's going to happen when they pull out?"

"The army's leavin'?" Drew asked.

"Some say if Kansas comes in as a free state, there will be trouble in the East, and they'll need more troops there."

"I reckon we'll just fend for ourselves then."

"You and your daddy against a whole band of Apaches?"

"All five of us shoot good," Drew bragged.

"Even your mother and sister?"

"They're the best shots in the family."

The man studied the adobe barn and then lowered his voice. "Say, son, do you folks have any saddle horses for sale? I'd like to buy one."

Drew looped his thumbs in his leather suspenders. "No, sir. Most are company horses. We aren't allowed to sell them. Me, my brother, and my sister each have our own horses, but they aren't for sale."

"I'll pay well," the man offered.

"No, sir, we ain't interested."

The man pushed back his hat and raised his eyebrows. "Fifty dollars."

Drew swallowed hard. "For a horse?"

"And a saddle, of course. What do you say?"

"Sorry, mister." Drew scratched his ear and started to walk away.

The man's voice was almost a whisper. "Do you mind if I talk to your sister and brother?"

"They don't want to sell either."

"Are you sure?"

"Hey, Talby . . . Blaze!" Drew shouted. "You want to sell your horse to this man for fifty dollars, including the saddle?"

The man's face flushed.

The shorter, unshaven passenger spun around, his hand on the grip of his revolver, which was shoved into his belt. "What do you think you're doin'?" he shouted.

"Just checkin' options," the man with the gray hat replied.

"My horse isn't for sale, mister," Blaze declared.

"Mine either," Talby said.

"You fixin' to leave the stagecoach?" Whap Martin called down to the man.

"Not now," the man with the gray hat replied as he crawled into the stage.

"That's good 'cause through tickets like yours can only be refunded by an agent, not a driver," Whap informed the man.

"I can't believe you tried to buy a horse without tellin' me," the shorter passenger mumbled as he climbed in the back.

Whap Martin tipped his hat. "Good-bye, Rand . . . Drew . . . Ceva . . . Miss Blaze . . . and wherever that young Talby is."

"Mr. Martin," Ceva Joyton called out. "Mr. Martin, who is the deceased man?"

"I got no idea in the world," the driver roared.

"You don't even know his name?"

"Nope. I heard he got on at El Paso. Said he was goin'

to Visalia. He was sleepin' when these two got on at Soldier's Farewell. See you on the return next week."

Whap shouted.

Six fresh horses bolted.

Hooves crashed.

And newly greased wheels rolled west over Sonora Pass.

Mr. Joyton ambled over to Drew. "We'd better dig a grave for this ol' boy."

"Where are we goin' to bury him, Daddy?"

"By the cottonwoods. It's the only spot in five miles where we can dig down over a foot. As far away from the spring as we can, of course."

"Rand, what would you like me to do?" Mrs. Joyton asked.

"You don't have to touch him if you don't want to."

"I don't mind," she told him.

"Whap said he thought the man got on without any belongings. We need to check his pockets and boots for personal effects."

"I'll do that." Mrs. Joyton nodded.

Rand Joyton handed a short-handled shovel to Drew.

"Darlin', sack up anything you think a wife or mother might want to keep. That's about all we can do. We don't have wood for a coffin."

It took Drew and his father an hour and a half to dig a grave several feet deep. Both were bare-chested and sweaty when they finished. They carried their shirts over their arms when they trudged back to the house.

Ceva Joyton waited for them in the shade of the porch.

"Did you find any personals, Mama?" Drew asked.

"A few. He had a ring, his pocket pistol, a folding knife in his boot, a very worn gold eagle, several silver dollars, and a bill of sale for a valise at Santa Fe."

"Whap said he didn't have a satchel," Mr. Joyton said.

"Just because he once bought a valise doesn't mean he had to have it on this trip," she replied.

"Is that all?" Mr. Joyton pressed.

"I thought it interesting that inside the right pocket of his coat were the initials H. W. in black India ink."

"H. W.?" Mr. Joyton asked.

"Do you think that's his initials, Mama?" Drew quizzed.

She stared down at the blanket-covered body. "I don't know. If he bought a used coat, they could be anyone's initials."

"Mama, I think this man was left-handed," Drew commented.

"Why do you say that?"

"Look at his shirt cuff on his left hand. It has old ink stains. Every time Daddy signs our name on the register at the Emerald Hotel in Tucson, he gets ink on his right cuff from others that have signed before him," Drew reported.

"My word, that's quite an observation." Mr. Joyton pulled his white cotton shirt over his head. "But I guess it doesn't matter much now."

"It might," Ceva Joyton said. "I checked that right suit coat pocket for personals, but all I found were the initials and a few hundred grains of black powder."

"That's where he carried that pocket pistol. I reckon Drew is correct. A left-handed man would keep his pistol in his right pocket."

"I studied the body, Daddy," Drew continued. "The man in the gray hat said this man pulled his gun out of his pocket and shot himself in the heart. If a man is left-handed and keeps his gun in his right pocket, he might pull out his gun and shoot himself in the right chest, but not in the heart." Drew demonstrated, making a gun with his fingers.

"What are you saying?" Mrs. Joyton asked.

"That man didn't shoot himself," Drew announced.

TWO

Drew was shoveling manure into an old wooden wheelbarrow the next morning when Blaze strolled up. "I put some wildflowers on Hadden Witherspoon's grave," she announced.

"Why Hadden Witherspoon?"

"Why not?" She stepped back as he tossed another shovelful into the two-wheeled wagon. "Drew, do you really think he was murdered?"

"I don't know, sis. I know it didn't happen like they said it did. And what reason do they have for lying except to cover something up?"

"Yes, that's what I think. I believe the three had stolen a gold shipment to Santa Fe. Hadden hid the funds and broke away from the other two. They caught up with him at Soldier's Farewell and tried to make him tell where the gold was buried."

"Wow, sis, that's quite a story."

"There's more." She beamed. "The one with the gray hat found out where the gold was, or the map was, or something like that, but the unshaven man didn't know he knew. Then they killed Hadden. The one with the gray hat wanted to secretly buy a horse from us so he could ride off and recover the gold."

"Which means the gold is within riding distance of here?"

"It's possible."

"Of course . . . the men might have gotten the story confused. What if Howie Wert did shoot himself by accident?"

"But that story is so boring! You think his name is Howie Wert?" she laughed.

"Why not?"

"Because his name is Hadden." Blaze peeked around the corrals. "Where's Talby?"

"Where do you think?"

"He went to fly a kite?"

"He says he dried the willow sticks next to the fireplace, and they were ready."

"Did he take Snickers?"

"Yep."

"Nobody flies a kite from horseback," she said.

"He's planning on being the first."

Blaze stepped closer. Her red braid reached down her back to the white lace sash around her waist. "Did you hear them howl again last night?" she whispered.

"Yes. Did you mention it to Mama?"

"No. Did you tell Daddy?"

"No. He just says there aren't any wolves around here, and it must be the coyotes."

"I'm not sure why only you and me can hear them."

"We're the only two that don't snore," Drew laughed.

"If Kite-Boy comes back, send him inside. Mama wants him to carry out the ashes and beat some rugs."

Drew finished his chores with his shirt lying over the fencepost. The June air was still, but clean and warm. The heat from the valley below crept up to Sonora Pass as usual. He knew it would cool off once the sun went down.

He heard the steady clang of the sledgehammer as his father beat out horseshoes on the anvil. His mother sat on the adobe wall and stared down the valley to the north.

"What're you thinkin' about, Mama?"

She took a deep breath. "I'm thinking how easy it is for me to breathe in this dry desert air. I haven't coughed in a month, and I was just thanking the Lord."

"It's a purdy view from up here, isn't it?"

"Yes. I considered bringing my sketchbook out and drawing this. What do you think, honey?"

"I think you ought to do it. You're very good at it, Mama."

"Do you know what's difficult? Trying to show how huge and empty this land is. Someday the West will fill up, and people won't remember how big and new and empty the land was."

"I don't reckon the Chiricahua Apaches think of this land as empty."

"You're right about that, Drew, but for the rest of us, we have to ride two hours in either direction to find a neighbor. We have to ride two days to find a town. That's what we call empty land."

"Talby said we might be going to town before the Fourth of July."

"That would be nice, but I'd rather not go without Daddy, and he needs to stay until they send someone reliable for relief. So it doesn't look too promising."

"I'll stay and help Daddy if you, Blaze, and Talby want to go to town."

"I like it when we all go together."

"I know, Mama, but Blaze is too purdy to be stuck up here in the pass her whole life."

"Oh, my, what a nice thing for a brother to say. Your daddy says sis is too purdy to take to town."

"He's just teasing, Mama."

"You're right about that. . . . Enough dawdling. I have quilts and blankets to hang, just in case little brother decides to do his chores."

Blaze stepped out on the porch. "Mama, there's a snake on the rafter in the boys' room. Where's the hoe?"

"How big is it, Blaze?" Drew asked.

"Not too big—maybe three or four feet."

"I'll get him. I'll salt his hide and make a hatband out of him. Travelers will pay a dollar for a rattlesnake hatband."

"The hoe is over by Henry Wellborn's grave," Ceva Joyton informed him.

"Is that what you call him, Mama?" Drew laughed. "Blaze thinks his name is Hadden."

"Perhaps it's Henry Hadden Wellborn," she offered. "Come on, sis, we need to pull the blankets and quilts. You might want to count chicks. If there's a rattler around here sleeping, it's because he's full."

"It better not have gotten one of Rhonda's chicks. She gets really melancholy when she loses one."

Drew shook his head. "Blaze, you're the only person I ever knew that worries about the emotions of chickens."

"Sounds silly, doesn't it? But it gives me something

to do. There aren't too many social activities for a sixteen-year-old up here."

Drew looked over at his mother and raised his eyebrows.

"Okay, you're right," Ceva replied.

"What's Drew right about?" Blaze asked.

"About skinning the rattlesnake and selling the hide. People are fascinated with the idea of owning a rattlesnake hide." Ceva Joyton took her daughter's arm. "By the way, I think you, me, and Talby will be going to Tucson before the Fourth of July."

Drew plucked up the hoe that leaned against the smallest cottonwood tree. He paused at the fresh mound of dirt.

Lord, it doesn't seem right that a person's life ends at a hole in the ground. But then it doesn't really end there, does it? I mean, there is heaven or hell. So I reckon the body stays in the ground awhile, but the soul beats it to one of those places. We have no idea where Mr. Howie Wert is. But You know. And You are fair and just. So I reckon he has no complaints right now.

He marched over to the forge as his father shoved a red-hot horseshoe into a bucket of water. A gray ball of smoke puffed into the clear blue Arizona sky.

"I need to borrow your one-pound hammer, Daddy."

Rand Joyton studied the hoe in Drew's hand. "You killin' snakes?"

"Yeah. Blaze said there's a nice-sized rattlesnake in the rafters of our bedroom. I figure to tan the hide and make a hatband."

"Tell Mama to cook the meat," Mr. Joyton instructed.

"I'll tell her."

"But don't let her put it in the stew. I hate to keep telling folks it's an 'assorted meat' stew."

"Maybe I'll pepper it and roast it right over the flames," Drew said.

"Bring it out here and use my fire. I wouldn't mind a little snack."

"Daddy, can I make a wooden headstone for the man we buried?"

"You mean ol' Hartley Whittaker?"

"Yeah, him. There ought to be some kind of marker, don't you think?"

"Sounds fine to me, son. Mama has some dry paint. You could mix up a batch and mark the date and his initials on the headstone even if we don't know his real name."

"I'll be right back."

"Now be careful this time, Drew," Mr. Joyton cautioned. "Your mama doesn't like a mess on the floor."

Drew stooped down and entered the big room of the stagecoach station. He meandered to the door in the southwest corner of the long adobe house. Curled around the cedar log rafter over his and Talby's bed was the diamondback.

"Mr. Snake, I know you appreciate this quiet, peaceful, cool room to sleep in. And I appreciate the contribution you are about to make to my purse and my stomach."

Drew raised the hoe an inch at a time. Then, with a snap of the wrist, flipped the startled snake to the wooden floor. He pinned the snake down with the flat part of the hoe, just behind its head. Scooting over, he gave the angry snake a quick tap on the head with the one-pound hammer.

It was a thorough tap.

Drew carried the hammer and hoe in his right hand and plucked up the tail of the dead snake next to the rattles. He hiked out into the big room, dragging the snake alongside him.

His mother had her arms loaded down with quilts. "Drew Joyton, don't drag that snake across my clean floor."

He raised his hand high enough so that the snake dangled straight down without touching the floor. "Sorry, Mama."

Blaze met him in the front yard. "I thought he was bigger than that."

"How's Rhonda?"

"She's happy. All the chicks are there. But I did notice a couple eggs missing this morning. Mr. Snake might have gotten them. But Gertie might have hidden her eggs behind the privy again. I didn't check."

Drew had the snake skin nailed down to a weather-beaten scrap of one-by-twelve and was roasting another bite for his father when Talby rode up. His paint horse had red silk flagging from its tail.

"You surely got Snickers all decorated up," Mr. Joyton laughed.

"We had an accident," Talby admitted.

"You mean, that's not how you fly a kite on horseback?" Drew teased.

"What're you cooking?" Talby asked.

"Rattlesnake. You want a bite?"

"Yeah."

Drew handed the wooden skewer to his brother. "Let it cool off a little."

Talby slid a bite off with his teeth. "Is this the one over our bed?"

"Did you know it was there?"

"I spied it when I woke up but forgot to mention it."

Rand Joyton rubbed his clean-shaven chin. "Son, why is that mirror hanging from your horse's tail?"

Talby swallowed a lump of snake meat. "Oh, that's hanging from the kite. I had a new idea. It's really quite marvelous. You see, I'll fly my kite five hundred feet in the air."

"Five hundred feet?" Drew questioned.

"Almost that much. Then I'll tilt this mirror on a forty-five-degree angle under the kite. I'll take another mirror down here and reflect the sunlight straight up to that little mirror, and it will beam my light out for fifty miles."

"Just exactly what is the purpose of that?" Drew asked.

Talby slid another big bite of snake meat into his mouth. "Simhmphnnlls," he mumbled.

"What?"

"Signals. We can signal up and down the trail from our position up here in Sonora Pass. It even works at night because I could use a lantern to create the light."

"There is one difficulty," Drew pointed out. "Getting a kite up in the air."

"If I had me that balsa wood, I could do it." Talby picked his teeth with his fingernail. "This bite was a little stringy."

"Talby, help your mama. She has chores for you," Mr. Joyton instructed.

"When you're done," Drew added, "Daddy said we can build a headboard for that man we buried."

"For Hamilton Washington?" Talby queried.

"That's the worst name anyone has thought of so far," Drew moaned.

"Thank you." Talby untied the silk kite from the horse's tail. "Daddy, did I remember to tell you that two tandem wagons are headed this way, pulled by six pair of oxen each?"

Mr. Joyton tossed down the sledge hammer and hiked out to the roadway. "I think you forgot to tell me that." He stared west. "There were only two tandems?"

Talby wiped his mouth on his sleeve. "Yep."

"Must be a short haul then. Tell your mother we'll have company for dinner. Drew, save the rest of this snake meat. We'll dump it in the stew after all. Bullwhackers aren't a choosy bunch."

From the time the slow-moving freight wagons were spotted in the west, it took almost two hours for them to reach Sonora Pass Station. Rand, Drew, and Talby Joyton stood alongside the road to greet them.

The first bullwhacker looked almost as wide as he was tall. His untrimmed gray beard flailed out in several directions. His axle-greaser looked about sixteen, with a smooth, tanned face.

"Ho to you folks," the bullwhacker called as he approached.

"Howdy and welcome," Mr. Joyton greeted them. "The wife's got dinner stirred and hot coffee poured. Me and the boys will see that your oxen get some water."

The bullwhacker parked the wagon in the middle of the road between the house and the corrals. He shoved his whip up in the front freight wagon.

"I'm Possum-Eatin' Summerfield. Most just call me Possum. This here kid is my help, Socrates Banyon."

The boy brushed back his light brown hair and ambled over to them. "They call me Tease."

"I'm Rand Joyton. These are my boys, Drew and Talby."

"You got tall boys, Joyton," Possum hooted.

"My sister is as tall as me," Drew reported.

Tease raised his thick eyebrows. "Where is she?"

Drew studied the boy's face. "In the dinin' room with Mama."

"I reckon I'm mighty hungry." Tease grinned.

The second tandem wagon rolled in. This bull-whacker was no more than five feet tall, but the muscles on his arms stretched his cotton shirt tight. He strolled up to where they stood. "Possum, toss me a chaw of tobaccy," he hollered, and then caught the object with one hand. "Howdy, folks. I'm Zink Chadron."

"This here is the Joytons. They run the station," Possum said.

"Have you got a helper too?" Drew asked.

"Nope. Tease is drawin' double pay and doin' a fine job. Ain't never seen a kid work any harder."

"They have dinner waitin' for us inside, Zink," Tease said.

"Where are you all headed with all of this freight?" Talby asked.

"Why, right here, of course." Zink pulled off his hat and scratched his matted black hair.

"What do you mean, right here?" Mr. Joyton asked.

Zink shoved his hat back on. "You didn't tell them, Possum?"

"I was jist gettin' ready to." Summerfield spat a big wad of tobacco out into the road. "This cargo is to be delivered to the store at Sonora Pass."

Mr. Joyton glanced at the freight wagons. "The what?"

"The store . . . the mercantile," Possum muttered.

"There isn't any store here," Drew declared.

"This is the Sonora Pass Station of the Butterfield Stage Lines, isn't it?" Zink asked.

"That it is, but we don't have a store here," Mr. Joyton said.

"You do now," Possum hooted.

Mr. Joyton folded his massive arms across his chest. "But I don't understand. We haven't received any such word. I'm afraid there's a mix-up."

"That might be," Zink sputtered, "but here's the invoice. Of course, the sweat smudged it a little. It says, 'Sonora Pass Station.'"

"What kind of goods do you have?" Drew asked.

"A little of everythin'. I'm haulin' beans, rice, flour, sugar, salt—mostly foodstuff," Zink explained. "Possum's got the dry goods and household supplies."

"And a tent," Possum added.

"A tent?" Mr. Joyton asked.

"A big, old twelve-foot by twenty-foot wall tent. Maybe they figured you'd put the store in there," Possum said.

"We can't have a store. We don't have any customers except the stage line and others traveling the road. We're lucky to see six people in a day this time of the year," Mr. Joyton reported.

"I'd buy some tobaccy if you was open for business,"

Possum offered. "After dinner we can set the tent up and unload it all in there."

"I think you ought to just take it all back. There has to be a mistake," Mr. Joyton asserted.

"Can't do that. We weren't paid for any farther than Sonora Pass. Besides, we have to be down at Sulphur Springs in two days. Some old boy thinks he found silver down there and wants us to haul it back to Tucson."

"I heard the Chiricahuas are kind of testy around there," Drew warned.

"Yep. We ain't exactly lookin' forward to it," Zink admitted. "But he's payin' us double; so I reckon we'll make the run."

"Talby, show the men into the dining room and then come on back and help your brother and me tend these oxen," Mr. Joyton called out.

Drew toted dual buckets of water to one string of oxen while his father did the same to the other. After ten minutes Talby returned and surveyed the huge freight wagons covered with dirty white canvas tarps.

"Are we really goin' to open a store?" Talby called out.

"At least until we find out what this is all about," Mr. Joyton replied.

"Who's goin' to run the store?" Talby asked.

"Since we don't have any customers, I don't suppose it matters. Think I'll put Blaze and Drew in charge," Mr. Joyton announced. "I'll make them co-managers."

"How about me?" Talby pressed.

"You're the assistant manager."

Talby crawled up on the wagon wheel. "Wow, Assistant Store Manager, and I'm only twelve. Do I get to take the money?"

"No."

Talby jumped down. "I didn't think so."

"Are you serious, Daddy?" Drew asked.

"Your mother and I surely don't have time. Until Butterfield figures this out, you and sis will be in charge of the goods."

"Are we goin' to set up the tent now?" Drew asked.

"No, I think we'll go eat. It'll take all of us, includin' those three inside, to get the tent set up and the wagons unloaded."

"Don't count much on Tease," Talby said.

"Why's that?" Drew asked. "Zink said he was a hard worker."

"'Cause he's stuck on Blaze tighter than a thistle on a wool sock," Talby reported.

"Blaze is taller than him," Drew pointed out.

"Don't seem to bother him much," Talby replied.

Mr. Joyton hiked over to his boys. "I don't suppose Blaze is aggravated by the attention."

"She was sayin' 'mercy me' a lot," Talby reported.

Mr. Joyton began to laugh. "Looks like sis found someone to practice her Georgia accent on."

"Blaze doesn't have a Georgia accent," Drew said.

Mr. Joyton put his arm around his son's shoulders. "I reckon she does now. Mr. Socrates Banyon has no idea of the trap he just stuck his foot into."

THREE

When the sun ambled out of New Mexico and broke across the clear blue Arizona sky the next morning, the teamsters and Socrates Banyon were long gone. Drew and Blaze huddled by the open front flap of the big tent.

"We need to make ourselves a sign," Blaze maintained. "If someone came through here, they couldn't tell this was a store."

"I can paint one when I make a headboard for Howie," Drew offered.

"I want it to read, Sonora Pass Mercantile: Blaze Joyton & Drew Joyton, Proprietors."

"That's a lot of words," he commented. "Couldn't we just put, Mercantile: Blaze & Drew Joyton, Proprietors?"

"I'd like Sonora Pass on it. We don't have any sign that says that. And Blaze and Drew makes us sound like we're married."

"The way Tease Banyon was traipsin' after you, I would have thought you'd be wantin' to get married any day."

"Him? He was . . . eh . . . you know," she stammered.

"Too short?"

"Yes, that's it," she grinned. "Too short and too pushy."

"Did he shove you?" Drew asked.

"It was a different kind of pushy. You go paint the sign. I'll start pricing things."

Drew scratched his head. "How do we know what to charge?"

"Daddy said to take the invoice and add 20 percent to everything. He doesn't know what they want to do, but that way the company will make some money. We just need to keep careful records of what sold and for how much."

Talby Joyton crawled down off the roof and trotted across the road toward them. "We got a string of prospectors and mules headed up from the east. They are at Deception Rock."

"How many?" Blaze questioned.

"I counted twenty-four horses and mules, but I think only eight men. Some were walkin'; so it was hard to count."

"Talby, you go help Mama. We might need to fix them all breakfast," Blaze instructed. "I need to look around and make sure I know what we have. We don't even have shelves. How can you have a store without shelves?"

"I'll go get Daddy. We'll have a lot of animals to tend if they stay and eat," Drew said.

"Where is he?" she asked.

"He took that sorrel pair for a ride. He says they've been acting snuffy ever since they wrecked at Mariposa Junction."

"Do you know what direction he headed?"

"West."

Within moments Drew had saddled his chestnut gelding, Carlos, and cantered down the trail. One hundred yards west of the station, the stage road crested at the top of the pass and gently sloped down into the Sonoran Desert. As far as Drew could see, there was nothing green. No trees. Not even sage.

And no cloud of dust.

If Daddy's down here, he must be a long ways away. There's always a dust devil when those big horses run.

Drew reined up and surveyed the horizon for 360 degrees.

Nothing unusual.

Nothing moving.

Nothing.

Except a distant column of smoke to the south. It was so far away it looked like a tiny gray thread on a quilt of light blue.

Drew was still staring south when he heard horses behind him. He spun Carlos around. Rand Joyton rode one sorrel bareback and held a lead rope on the other.

"You reckon that's more than a campfire?" he asked his father.

"Yep, I do."

"Sulphur Springs is down there somewhere."

"I think it's farther south," Mr. Joyton said.

"How far away do you think that smoke is?"

"In this desert air could be fifty miles."

"Mama's right. This is open land. A column of smoke within fifty miles, and we spot it." Drew stared at the two horses. "I didn't see you on the road."

"I took them over to the sand dunes. St. Paul was a bit testy; so I made them work a little. What are you doin' down here?"

"Daddy, we got a string of prospectors headed up the grade. Figured you would want to know."

Mr. Joyton rubbed his chin. "You're right, son. Let's trade. You bring St. Peter and St. Paul. I'll ride Carlos. That way I can get back sooner."

Drew slid down out of the saddle and offered his horse to his father. Mr. Joyton held both big stage horses while Drew grabbed St. Peter's mane and pulled himself up.

"Blaze has the store open, Daddy, but I haven't got a sign painted."

"It will do. I doubt if anyone will ride through here without asking what's in the tent."

Drew rode up the slope and watched his father crest the pass and drop out of sight. The road zigzagged up the treeless mountain, and Drew rode at a walk. When he reached Faraway Perch, he stopped and stared south, but he could no longer see the column of smoke.

A howl to the north of him sent goose bumps down his back. A second wolf howl came from the south. He urged the horses to a trot.

Wolves don't howl in the middle of the day. Drew refused to look north or south but rode the big horses up the road to the east. *I'm not afraid. It was just an animal or two. I'll be home in a minute. The Lord will take care of me. I should have brought my shotgun. Lord, I don't know why I get scared when I don't even know if there's anything out there. Well, something's out there. But I don't know for sure if it's man or beast. Even if there are Chiricahuas this close, it doesn't mean they're plannin' to harm me. They could just be . . . wanting . . . to . . . eh . . . buy some cornmeal at the store. Or . . . or . . . slit my throat and steal the horses.*

Drew jammed his heels into the big sorrel. Both horses broke into a gallop.

He didn't hear any more wolves.

And he didn't slow down until he crested the pass and looked down on the station. Sixteen mules and eight horses were tied to a rope stretched tight between the corral and the nearest cottonwood tree. Mr. Joyton was hauling water to the animals.

Drew rode up to his dad. "You want me to help you, Daddy?"

"Go help your sister. The store is a popular spot."

Drew turned the stagecoach horses out and trotted over to the big tent. Five men and one redheaded girl rummaged through the sacks, crates, and barrels.

"You got any salt pork, Missy?"

"Hack, did you say you saw some black powder?"

"I said black pepper. There's a fifty-pound sack of black pepper over here."

"That's too much."

"Ray, I didn't mean buyin' the whole sack."

"Here's a tin of soda crackers, boys. This one is mine."

"If we don't find an axe handle, we'll be cuttin' firewood with our teeth!"

"There's some .50-caliber lead balls, but I don't see any .45-caliber."

"Buy the .50s. We'll use my mold and melt them down."

Drew scooted up behind Blaze. "What can I do, sis?"

"Isn't this crazy? We open a store in a tent in the middle of the wilderness, and someone found it already." She clapped her hands. The men stopped scrounging. "Men, this is my brother Drew. He's the other proprietor. He'll help you find things. We're going to use that plank on those barrels for a counter. You can pay me for the goods there. Any questions?"

"Is your sis married, Drew?" one of the men shouted.

"You got any other sisters?" another asked.

"Any shorter ones?" a third man hooted.

"Does she shoot a gun?"

Blaze shook her head. "You men have been in the mountains too long."

"Yes, Miss Blaze, you're right about that."

A tall man with a beard halfway down his chest meandered to the plank counter. "We're pullin' out in five minutes, boys. That new gold strike is beckonin'."

As the men finished gathering supplies, Drew sidled up to his sister. "Where did you find this plank?"

"The yardage was stacked on it."

"We have bolts of cloth?" Drew asked.

"Fifty."

"This makes a great counter."

She wrote down each item the man purchased. "I had to think of something in a hurry."

Drew toted a twenty-five-pound sack of beans out behind the men. "Where are you headed?" he asked.

"Sulphur Springs. There's a new strike down there, we hear."

"I've heard the same thing," Drew said.

"Are there many down there yet?"

"Not that I know of. Only one outfit and some teamsters. But keep an eye out. I saw a column of smoke in that general direction about an hour ago. Nobody burns a fire that big in daylight on purpose."

"You think there are Indians down there?"

"I think there are Indians right on the other side of Sonora Pass," Drew warned.

The man stared at him, then took a deep breath. "A man will take a lot of chances to get rich, son." He stared across the yard where Mrs. Joyton visited with another of the prospectors. "Foolish chances maybe. You're rich, son. No need for you to take chances."

Drew shrugged. "We don't have very much."

"You got ever'thin'. You got a hard-workin' daddy and a purdy mama. You got a redheaded sis and a little brother. You got a dry bed at night and fresh air to breathe in the mornin'. You got food on your table and a tall, strong body. Yep, son, you got ever'thin'."

Drew hiked back to the store as the men spurred their string of mules and horses up over the pass. Blaze stood at the counter. "We have nine dollars and two pinches of gold. What is gold selling for?"

"I think it's fourteen dollars a pinch. I don't know for sure."

"If so, that's thirty-seven dollars."

"That makes $7.40 profit," he figured.

"Daddy assumes Butterfield will want half the profit. We get to split the rest."

Drew rocked back on the heels of his dirty black boots. "That's $1.85 each, and we only worked about an hour!"

"It took us four hours to set this up yesterday and over an hour before they got here. We've put in six hours for that $1.85. That's almost 31 cents an hour," Blaze corrected.

"Which is 31 cents an hour better than yesterday."

Drew plucked up a silver dollar, flipped it in the air, and caught it. "I like the store business."

Blaze strolled around the merchandise. "We need a building, shelves, a door, and a storeroom."

The silver dollar bounced off Drew's fingernail, plopped on the packed dirt, and rolled under the counter. Drew dropped to his knees and fished it out.

"It's a sign!" he shouted.

Blaze hurried over to her brother. "A dropped quarter is a sign?"

"No, the counter. This big plank is a sign. There's writing on the other side."

"What does it say?" she asked.

"Something about a mercantile. I think it says, Sonora Pass Mercantile."

"That's our sign. They did have one!" Blaze called out. "Quick, help me turn it over."

They turned the sign over and studied it.

"Sonoma Pass? This isn't Sonoma Pass," she mumbled.

"Who's Blair Drakeville?" Drew asked. "Daddy was right. They shipped this stuff to the wrong place."

Talby burst into the tent. "Did you find any balsa wood?"

"Not yet, but we found this sign," Blaze announced.

Talby studied it. "Sonoma Pass Mercantile: Blair A. Drakeville, Proprietor." He laced his fingers on top of his head. "Maybe someone changed the name of this pass."

By the time the eastbound stage rolled down the pass into the station, the sign had been changed to read, "SonoRa Pass Mercantile: BlaZE AND DrEW JOYTON,

ProprietorS. The passengers were ushered into the station house for dinner where Blaze assisted her mother. Drew helped his father switch teams.

The Assistant Manager ran the store. Talby stood in the big tent and peered out at his brother. "I don't have any customers," he complained.

"You see how nice a job you have? You aren't bothered by customers," Drew laughed.

"Is this the only time I get to run the store?"

"Someday you'll get a customer."

"I could sit on the roof with the telescope and tend the store."

"You want to trade with Drew?" Mr. Joyton asked.

"No. Doin' nothin' is better than doin' some things."

They had just finished harnessing the fresh team when the driver, Royce Purline, meandered out of the station.

"I reckon you heard about that ol' boy on the westbound yesterday," he blurted out.

Drew pointed to the cottonwoods. "He's buried right over there."

"Who's buried right over there?" Royce asked.

"The guy who died on the westbound."

"They brought the body back here?"

"He was in the coach when they pulled in," Mr. Joyton said.

Purline scratched his neck. "Who was in the coach?"

"The guy buried over there," Drew insisted.

"Are we talkin' about the same guy?"

Mr. Joyton leaned on the rump of the wheel horse. "The man who got on the westbound at El Paso and reportedly shot himself."

"I didn't hear that one," Purline said.

"What are you talkin' about, Royce?" Mr. Joyton asked.

"One of the passengers fell out of the stage at Arroyo Diablo."

"Fell out?"

"J. J. said he got sick and leaned his head out the door window to vomit. Door swung open, and he tumbled all the way to the bottom of the arroyo. They sent some men out to get the body. It was too steep for Whap and J. J."

"Which man?" Drew asked. "One with a new gray hat? Or the other—"

"It was the other man."

Mr. Joyton pulled out his red bandanna and wiped his neck. "One man accidentally shot himself, and another got sick and fell out?"

"J. J. said it was a strange trip. I hadn't heard about this guy. They were busy giving a report to the deputy U.S. Marshal. I figured it was just about the one who fell out."

"Did you happen to hear the name of the man with the gray hat?" Drew asked the stagecoach driver.

"Nope," Purline replied. "But I know the name of the man who fell out of the stagecoach. His name was Harold Weston, but he was called Pinch."

"Harold Weston?" Drew choked. "He's H.W.?"

Rand Joyton pulled off his hat and scratched his head; then he pointed out to the grave by the cottonwoods. "We thought the old boy we buried was H.W. We found those initials on his coat. But maybe he had borrowed the other man's jacket."

"Or the one who fell out of the stagecoach had borrowed this man's name," Drew surmised.

"Now you've got me really confused." Purline shook his head. "You got any tobacco in the store?"

"Yep," Mr. Joyton replied. "Drew, you go take care of him."

"What about me?" Talby called out.

Mr. Joyton waved at the chimney. "You get on the roof and scout the road."

Talby stomped through the yard. "Bein' Assistant Manager isn't what I thought it was goin' to be."

Rhonda and her chicks scurried to the shade at the west end of the station.

Drew led Royce Purline to the store and watched as the man counted out coins to pay for the brick of tobacco.

"Mr. Purline, when you came over the pass, did you hear any wolves on the west side?" Drew asked.

"Wolves? There ain't any wolves around here."

"That's not what I asked. I asked if you heard any?"

"With those squeakin' wheels, son, I couldn't hear a wolf if it was ridin' shotgun. You hear wolves?"

"My sister and I can hear them sometimes. I figure it's Chiricahua Apache."

"Could be. Thanks for the warnin'. We'll keep extra vigil." Royce Purline glanced around the crowded tent. "You don't happen to have any yardage, do you? My wife told me to pick up some gingham in Tucson, and it slipped my mind."

"Purple, green, blue, or red?" Drew asked.

"Red."

"We have a whole bolt of it."

"Not anymore." Purline grinned.

Blaze joined Drew as two of the passengers peered into the store.

"You have a lot of goods out here," a man wearing a silk top hat and six-day beard proclaimed.

"It's a new store," she replied.

"It's inspiring. I write for *Harper's Magazine*. Two teenagers willing to take a gamble and open a store in the middle of nowhere would make a good story."

"It wasn't our idea," Blaze explained. "It was kind of thrust upon us. It's a Butterfield company store."

"At least, we think it is," Drew said.

"Yes, but you were up to the challenge. In the midst of Apache aggression, a lonely outpost stands as a vestige of civilization." He marched out to the stagecoach.

Within minutes the Celerity wagon rumbled east in a cloud of dust.

"I always wanted to be a vestige of civilization." Drew grinned.

"Some people wait their whole life to be a vestige of civilization," Blaze giggled.

"Someday I hope to become a credit to my community."

"You aren't a debit, are you?"

"No, more like a push. How about you, Blaze? What's your goal?"

"I'd like to be the Princess of the Prairie, or the Duchess of the Desert, or perhaps the Angel of Arizona!" she snickered.

Drew burst out laughing. "I love it. Blaze, you're a great sister."

She hugged his shoulder. "We make a good team, don't we?"

"I reckon we do."

"I have to go help Mama with the dishes."

"I'll tote you some fresh water."

"Let's go for a ride this evening, Drew. I haven't ridden Sage in almost a week."

"If we aren't too busy with the store."

"We might have one of the only stores in Arizona where you can see potential customers for fifty miles before they get here." Drew watched as Blaze sashayed back to the house. She swooped down, plucked up Rhonda, and carried the hen to the step.

Drew plodded over to the spring by the cottonwoods.

Lord, I don't know if every brother feels this way, but when it comes time for me to marry, I surely would like to find a girl like my sister. She's smart and fun, and she makes me want to try my hardest, and it seems to me that's good. Now I don't reckon my girl should have red hair 'cause then she'd have to compete with Mama and Blaze, and that wouldn't be fair to any girl.

He stopped by the grave.

"Mr. H.W., now we find out you might not be H.W. You're surely a mystery man."

Something caught Drew's attention. He stared at the fresh dirt. "Footprints! Someone has been walkin' over his grave with bare feet!"

FOUR

Drew carried a steaming enameled tin cup of coffee across the road toward the corrals as the eastern sky turned from black to slate gray. Mr. Joyton sat on a piece of a log stitching a broken harness.

"Mornin', Daddy. Mama sent you this."

"Thanks, son."

"Did you get any sleep?"

"Not too much, but that wasn't because of visitors. Not too comfy sitting in the dirt, leanin' against the corral."

"So there was nothing suspicious?" Drew asked.

"Nope."

"You figure those were Indian tracks on the grave?"

Mr. Joyton let the coffee steam his face. "Yep. Unless one of you kids has been sleepwalkin' barefoot."

Drew squatted down next to his father. "Talby talks a lot in his sleep and sometimes sits up, but I've never seen him walking around."

"I studied the tracks. I think the person hiked to the springs and just happened to go across the fresh dirt."

Drew glanced back toward the cottonwoods. "What're we goin' to do?"

"I'll probably sleep out here one more night." Mr. Joyton stretched his arms out to his side. "But we can't deny folks water, no matter who they are. If they don't bother us, we won't bother them."

"Blaze slept with her revolver under her pillow," Drew reported.

"How about you?"

"The shotgun was lyin' between me and Talby. It's the first night he's stayed on his side of the bed and not kicked me in a month."

"You plannin' on usin' it every night?" Mr. Joyton grinned.

"I was thinkin' about it. Daddy, do you think it's safe for me and Blaze to go for a ride this mornin' after chores? We wanted to last night, but with these footprints we decided against it."

"If you ride east. That way you can stay within sight of the station. Take your shotgun, of course."

"Will the store be all right?"

"I reckon Talby will watch it just fine. Your mama and me will look after it if we need to. No stage is due for two days. But we never know what will come our way."

Talby was pouring hot white gravy over his fried eggs and biscuits when Drew stooped at the doorway and entered the station. Blaze sat at the end of the huge table, two fried eggs staring up at her.

"Daddy said we could go for a ride after chores," Drew called out.

She clapped her hands. "Good! Perhaps we can beat the heat."

"What about me?" Talby asked.

"You get to run the store," Drew explained.

"You mean you don't expect any customers?"

"Something like that."

"I may as well go for a ride with you." Talby jabbed more biscuits and white gravy into his mouth.

"Sure," Blaze said. "Check with Daddy."

Six wagons with Mexican miners rolled through Sonora Pass about 8:00 A.M. They passed on breakfast but drank coffee and bought the brightest yardage in the store and a fifty-pound sack of cornmeal. None of the group spoke English, but they smiled their way through the transaction and left, taking a trail to the southeast.

Drew saddled Carlos, but Blaze and Talby rode bareback.

Drew carried his shotgun across his lap.

Blaze stuck her revolver in her dress pocket.

Talby toted a rebuilt red silk kite.

They rode east along the road toward Washburn Creek. The road went straight down the mountainside and only dipped once or twice. The eastern slope of the mountain, like the western slope, was treeless and grassless. Only yucca, sparse sage, and huge boulders broke up the landscape.

"Mama's straw hat looks nice on you," Drew said.

"She said I couldn't go riding without a hat or bonnet. I wasn't about to wear a bonnet. What if we meet someone? I would die of embarrassment."

Talby glanced over at Drew. "Who are we goin' to meet?"

Drew surveyed the desert to the east and north. "Just because we can see fifty miles doesn't mean we won't have visitors. Maybe some handsome men are hidin' behind these rocks, just waitin' for the Delight of the Desert, the Angel of Arizona . . ."

Blaze stuck out her tongue.

"Let's ride down to Cactus Flats," Talby suggested. "I want to show you how high this kite will fly."

"He's quite an optimistic fellow," Blaze laughed. She turned Sage off the trail. "Come on, let's race."

The slope now was gradual, unlike the steep descent at the station.

The dirt was dry, soft.

The three raced head-to-head half the way down; then Snickers slowed. Talby dropped back. Blaze was a step ahead when they reached the barranca at Washburn Creek.

Sage stopped.

Carlos leaped over it.

Drew reined him up and waited for the other two to catch up.

"Sage is too old to jump that far. Oh, I think he could do it, but he couldn't remember why he should," she laughed.

"Snickers said she wanted to rest," Talby shouted as he approached.

"Maybe she's too tired to fly a kite," Drew hollered back.

Talby trotted up.

"Do you think there's enough of a breeze to fly a kite?" Blaze asked.

"That's the beauty of my kite design. It's designed to fly even when the wind isn't strong."

Drew glanced over at Blaze, then back at Talby. "Tell

me again, why don't you get off your horse, run across the prairie, get your kite in the air, and then climb back on the horse?"

"Oh, sure, that's what everyone does."

"They do?"

"And most everyone sleeps with their eyes closed, but that doesn't make it bad," Blaze argued.

"Look," Talby explained, "the worst thing about flying a kite is all that running to get it up in the air. Now, Snickers likes to run. So why not use her enthusiasm to get the kite airborne?"

"You sold me, little brother," Drew conceded. "Go fly your kite. We'll watch from here."

"I need one of you to help. Every time I try it, the kite drops down and gets caught in Snickers's tail. So if one of you would hold the kite back there about twenty feet and then toss it in the air as soon as I gallop off, I'd have a better chance to get it up."

"Which way are you riding?" Blaze asked.

"West, so the sun isn't in my eyes."

"But the wind is driftin' from the east. Wouldn't that be better?" Drew suggested. "Of course, everyone does it that way. You might want to try it with the wind at your back."

"Very funny," Talby pouted.

"I'll hold your kite," Blaze offered. "Do you want me to get down?"

"No, I think the higher up you are, the better."

Blaze took the red silk kite from Talby. "In that case . . ." She rode back twenty feet, then turned Sage around. She swung her feet under her and stood straight up on Sage's back.

"Do I toss it or what?"

"Hold it very gently and let me tug it from your hand."

Straddling the paint filly, Talby held the string high above his head. "Count me down, Drew."

"Three . . . two . . . one . . . . go!"

Talby kicked Snickers. The horse bolted.

The kite yanked out of Blaze's hand and sailed straight up above Talby's head.

"It worked!" Talby shouted.

"Let out the string," Drew hollered.

Talby kept galloping as the kite rose higher and higher.

Blaze dropped down on Sage's back as Drew rode over to her. "I reckon we'd better keep up with Kite-Boy."

They trotted across the desert.

"I can't believe he actually got it up in the air," Drew said.

"How much string does he have?"

"I don't know, but it's getting up there."

They caught up with Talby on the rim of a sandy, dry creek bed.

"I did it," Talby shouted.

"Yes, you did. It's amazing," Blaze replied.

"I wish I had my mirrors set up. We could signal for miles."

"Who would you signal?" Drew asked.

"Eh . . . Mama. If she was sitting out on the patio sketching, I could signal her."

"What do we do now?"

"Why don't we just stay here awhile and let me fly this beauty. I hate to reel it in already."

"Can we all scoot down to those boulders? There's some shade down there," Blaze suggested.

"Sure, but I'm not crawlin' off Snickers. This is a horse-flown kite," Talby insisted.

"That's fine. I got some jelly biscuits that sis made in my saddlebags," Drew said.

Talby stared up at the kite. "It takes two hands to do this."

Drew winked at Blaze. "That's all right. There'll probably be some left."

They rode to the boulders. Blaze slid to the ground. Drew handed her the cotton sack out of his saddlebag and climbed down, shotgun in hand. Both horses stood still the moment their reins were dropped to the desert floor.

"I should have brought a lap quilt for our picnic," Blaze said.

"It ain't much of a picnic," Talby called down. "Just jelly biscuits."

"And ham," Blaze added.

"You didn't tell me that."

"Mama stuck in some ham."

"And raisins," Drew said.

"Raisins!" Talby's shoulders slumped. "That's no fair."

"Tie the string to your wrist and come down and eat with us," Blaze suggested.

Talby shoved his slouch hat back. "No, this has to be horseback-flown."

"Then tie it to the halter. Snickers isn't goin' anywhere without Sage and Carlos," Drew urged.

"Yeah, that would work." Talby tied the string to Snickers's halter and then watched the kite for a while.

Drew plopped down on the dirt in the shade of the rocks, a slab of ham in his hand. "Aren't you goin' to sit down, sis?"

"I don't want to sit in the dirt with this dress. I should have worn my old one."

Drew slipped his suspenders off his shoulders. Then holding the ham between his teeth, he pulled off his cotton shirt and spread it down beside him. "Here, sis!"

"Oh, my, how gallant." Blaze sat down cross-legged next to him. "You spoil me, Drew."

"That's not true."

Talby moseyed over, licking strawberry jam off a biscuit. "Aren't you goin' to pull off your trousers so I'll have a place to sit?"

Drew stuck out his tongue at his brother.

Talby plopped down on the dirt and leaned against the boulder.

Blaze broke off a bite of biscuit and popped it into her mouth. "Mama and I were talking about it yesterday."

"About what?" Drew pressed.

"Isn't that a beautiful sight?" Talby pointed to the kite in the sky. "I bet you can see it for miles."

"About how I'm spoiled by the men around me," Blaze continued.

"What do you mean?"

Talby squinted. "I read in a book that the Chinese make their kites to look like dragons. Wouldn't that be something? To look up and see a dragon floating above the desert?"

Blaze rolled a raisin in her fingers before she ate it. "Mama asked me what I thought of Tease Banyon."

"What did you tell her?"

Talby reached in the sack for another jelly biscuit. "I could make a bigger kite if I had my balsa wood. It's so light the kite just about floats on its own. I read about it in that old magazine Whap Martin left."

Blaze brushed down her skirt. "I said, 'He's not like Drew or Daddy; so I'm not interested.'"

"You said that?"

Talby stuffed half a biscuit into his mouth. "Dommmmpht whww numbly hanhptht squibmomth."

"Yes, I did. I want a boy who will pull off his shirt so I don't have to sit in the dirt, a boy who lets me be me and likes it. A boy who works hard and treats all women and girls with respect. I want a boy who is strong and brave and still gets down on his knees every night and says his prayers."

"Sounds like me, sort of," Drew mumbled.

"You see, Drew Joyton, that's what I mean—you spoiled me."

Talby gulped down the biscuit. "If I cut that kite loose, do you think it would blow all the way to Tucson?"

Drew studied the red object in the sky. "Nope, but it might go a mile or two."

They shared Drew's canteen of water.

Talby lay back against the rock to study the distant kite. "Do you think a person could make a big enough kite that he could hold onto it and fly with it?"

"How would he get in the air to start with?" Drew asked.

Talby waved his arms as he talked. "You could jump out of a hot-air balloon with a kite strapped to your back."

"Not me," Drew laughed. "I jumped off that bridge

into Emerald Lake up in Colorado. That's as high as I want to be, and it wasn't more than twenty feet."

"Maybe someone could jump off a bridge or cliff and have a team of fast horses down below . . . hmm . . . a train!" Talby shouted. "I'll go back to the States and build this big kite out of red silk and balsa wood. I'll have this five-hundred-foot rope hanging down from a tall bridge to the side of the track. Then when the train roars by under the bridge where I'm waiting, someone at the back of the train would grab my rope and dally it to the caboose. When the rope gets to the end, I'll leap up in the air and fly."

Drew glanced over at Blaze. "We should never let him get around a train."

"I'm not goin' to try it right away," Talby muttered.

"That's a relief."

"I'd have to say," Blaze remarked, "little brother is right about one thing. It would be such fun to soar way up in the air like an eagle or hawk. Sometimes on a windy day, I let my hair down and just go out and wave my arms and lean into the breeze."

"I like sailing up in a tall swing and then leaning back. I close my eyes and pretend to fly," Drew said.

"Why don't we put up a swing at Sonora Pass?" Blaze suggested.

"We only have three trees, and they're over by the springs," Talby said, his eyes closed now.

"Did you ever go over to Dog Manley's house in Tucson?" Drew asked.

Blaze laughed. "No. I never got used to calling a boy Dog."

"The center beam in their roof came straight out for

about ten feet past the house. They sank a log pole to support that end and hung a swing there."

"Did it work?"

"Yep, as long as no one wanted to go in or out the front door."

"We could do that. Our door is on the side."

"It wouldn't be very high," Talby said.

"But it would be a swing, and we could look over the whole valley when we're swinging," Blaze countered. "We have rope in the store."

"And there's a couple of poles out by the corrals that never got used for a barn. I don't know if they're long enough, but we could check on it."

"Oh, yes . . . a swing." Blaze sacked the extra food. "Let's go build it right now."

"I'm still flyin' my kite," Talby protested.

Drew surveyed the sky. "How much string did you have on that thing?"

"Only three hundred feet," Talby answered.

"It looks farther away than that," Drew observed.

Talby jumped up. "Where's Snickers?"

Drew stood up and offered his hand to Blaze.

"There she is," Talby shouted. He sprinted out on the desert floor.

Drew put on his shirt, and he and Blaze both mounted their horses.

"I reckon we should go rescue Kite-Boy," he laughed.

They trotted out on the yellow-brown barren dirt where Talby was chasing the paint horse, who kept a hundred feet in front of him.

"This was a really fun morning, Drew."

"Sis, do you think we're simple people?"

"What do you mean, simple?"

"We like simple things like riding horses. Or picnics. Or a swing."

"It feels good deep down inside, and we don't have to ask forgiveness at night. If that's simple, I like it."

"Yeah . . . me too. Did you know that Maggie DeShields told me I wouldn't ever amount to anything because I'm too simple?"

"She did? You haven't seen Maggie in seven years."

"There are some things a person doesn't forget." Drew stood in the stirrups. "Look, there's a wagon!"

"By Talby?"

"Headed toward him. See that column of dust? It's moving fast."

Drew held the shotgun as they raced toward Talby and Snickers. By the time they reined up, their brother was visiting with a man and woman in a large covered wagon.

Talby glanced up. "I'm a sign from the Lord." He grinned.

"What?" Blaze choked in the dust.

The woman took off her bonnet and fanned herself. "We were lost and were praying for deliverance."

"We were not lost," the man insisted. "We just got off the trail—that's all."

"We've been off the trail for a week."

"That's not true, Mother. We just took a little side trip out of Santa Fe."

"We were wanderin' in circles until we saw your brother's kite," the woman insisted.

The man pointed south. "Tucson is a few miles that way, correct?"

Drew pointed west. "Tucson is ninety-four miles in that direction."

"Ninety-four?" the man gulped.

"Ninety-four from our place. We live up there at the pass." Blaze pointed to the mountain.

"But the California stagecoach road is just a few miles south of there," Drew added.

"Praise the Lord!" the woman exclaimed. "I just knew that kite was an answer to prayer. Whoever heard of a kite in the desert? The Lord is good to the lost and destitute."

"We were not lost and are hardly destitute," the man grumbled.

"We're headed back to the stagecoach station where we live. Would you like to follow along?" Drew offered.

"Don't want to hold you back, son," the man replied. "You go on. We'll find it."

"We most certainly would like to follow along," the woman snapped. "I'm not letting these three out of my sight until we find that stage road. The girls and I have no intention of spending another night lost in the desert."

Drew surveyed the wagon. "You have girls?"

"Oh, yes," the woman said. "Let me introduce them. Nancy is fifteen."

A soft voice filtered from behind the canvas wagon flap. "Hi!"

"Eh, hello," Drew gulped.

"Natalie is our blonde-haired girl. She's fourteen."

The voice was sweet. Tentative. "Hi, everyone."

"Hi, Natalie," Blaze called out.

"And the baby just turned thirteen. She's Nellie."

A round face with bonnet pulled low appeared from

behind the wagon flap. "Hello," she said, then disappeared behind the flap in a chorus of giggles.

"The girls are a little shy," the lady offered.

Drew yanked off his hat. "Yes, ma'am, I noticed that. I'm Drew Joyton. I'm fourteen. You met my brother Talby, who's twelve. This is my sister Blaze. She's sixteen."

"What a wonderful name," the woman said. "Young Talby is quite tall for twelve. I thought him older."

"He's the shortest in the family," Drew stated. "Where are you folks headed?"

"To California," the man replied.

"You goin' to look for gold?"

"We're going to run a store, but I hear it's in gold country."

"We got a store up at the station," Talby blurted out.

"You don't say. Well, ours is at Sonoma Pass."

Drew stared at Blaze. "Sonoma Pass?" he mumbled.

"Yes, in California," the woman reported.

Drew felt his mouth drop.

"Oh, dear," she continued, "we didn't introduce ourselves. I'm Naomi. This is my husband, Blair. We're the Drakevilles."

FIVE

Drew hoisted the posthole digger handles above his head and slammed them back into the packed dirt of the station yard. He was digging halfway between the house and the low adobe wall. He had his shirt off, and his suspenders rubbed his shoulders.

Blaze strolled out to him. "How's it coming?"

"It's just hard dirt, but it feels like solid rock." Sweat trickled down the middle of his back.

"How deep is the hole?"

Drew paused and stared at the hole, then let out a big sigh. "About two feet."

"How deep should it be?"

He could smell his sister's lavender perfume. "Daddy said three to four feet, or as deep as I can go with this posthole digger."

"Drew, it'll be so wonderful to have a swing. How come we didn't think of it before?"

"'Cause you and me don't get to visit in private very much. We always have good ideas when we get a chance to discover them."

Blaze glanced across the road at the dusty white tent. "Have you seen the girls yet?"

He rubbed his arm across his mouth. It tasted salty. "Nope. As far as I know, they're still in the wagon or the store."

"What did they decide after I went to bed?" Blaze asked.

"Mr. Drakeville wanted to press on to California, but Mrs. Drakeville said she wasn't goin' one mile farther until he contacts Butterfield."

Blaze took the posthole digger from his hands. "So they're staying?"

"Mr. Drakeville said half those goods need to be sold here. They would never keep bein' shipped to California. So he agreed they would set up shop, just like they would have done there, and wait for the company to move them." He stepped back away from the hole.

"And just like that, you and me are out of the store business." She stepped over and peered into the dark hole. Her red braid hung down her back to her waist.

"We'll have more time to swing," he laughed.

"It does seem strange to have another family here." She raised the posthole digger handles above her head and slammed them down at the hole.

"Mama said it would be nice to have others to visit with, but I don't know if we'll ever see the Drakeville girls," Drew said.

Blaze tried to jerk the digger out of the hole, but it wouldn't budge. "Oh, Drew, are you anxious to see girls?"

Drew felt his face flush. He reached over, twisted the handles, and pulled the digger straight up with half a load of reddish yellow dirt. "I just want to be neighborly."

Blaze clapped her hands and laughed. "Oh, yes, we

must be neighborly. Why don't you and I go for a visit after a while. They have to receive us sometime. I'll bake them an apple pie."

"And I'll dig a round, deep hole. Daddy is forgin' the bolts and straps for the swing. If we can hoist that beam, we should have a swing by evenin'."

"May I have the first turn?"

"Yep. You're the reason I'm doin' all this."

Blaze wiggled her nose. "You see, Drew Joyton, I was right. You do spoil me."

"I just figured it's the way I'm supposed to treat all girls." He examined the reddened calluses on the palms of his hands.

"Only the ones that come out of their wagon." Blaze scampered back into the house.

Drew had punched the hole six inches deeper and felt the sweat burning into his eyes when Talby climbed off the roof of the stage station. "Some of them Mexicans are comin' back up the trail."

Drew stopped and stared toward the southwest. "Are you sure it's the same ones? They just left yesterday mornin'. They can't make it home and back so soon."

"Well, it's them," Talby insisted.

"Go tell Mama." Drew tossed down the posthole digger. "I'll tell Daddy."

Drew, Mr. Joyton, and Mr. Drakeville met four Mexican wagons as they rolled into Sonora Pass. All six men had on wide-brimmed black sombreros. The tallest had the longest beard. He spoke several sentences in Spanish.

Mr. Drakeville answered him.

"You know Spanish, Blair?" Mr. Joyton queried.

"A fair amount. We ran a store in Sherman, Texas, before movin' back up to Missouri."

"What did he say?" Mr. Joyton asked.

"There's Apache trouble to the south. The others returned to Socorro, but these want to wait here before crossing the Animas Valley and going home."

"They're welcome to stay," Mr. Joyton declared.

Mr. Drakeville nodded. "They said they'd work for meals."

"Work?" Mr. Joyton pulled off his gray slouch hat and scratched his head. "What do they do?"

Drakeville spoke with the men for several minutes. Then he turned to Mr. Joyton and Drew. "They're carpenters and adobe men."

Mr. Joyton shoved his hat back on. "They build houses?"

"Apparently so." Drakeville stood shorter than Drew but just as square-shouldered. "And stores."

"Stores?" Drew questioned.

"I just made a deal for them to build an adobe store," Drakeville announced.

"You what?" Mr. Joyton asked.

"I told them I'd feed and house them and give them each a bolt of cloth if they would work on building a modest store while they waited for the Apache trouble to end."

Rand Joyton surveyed the hillside. "You think the company wants you to build a store at Sonora Pass?"

"I have no idea. But these men need something to do. It's better that they feel like they're workin' for meals than to get them for nothing. The worst that can happen is that we're sent on, and you're left with an extra building."

"That sounds fair enough." Mr. Joyton nodded.

"I expect you and me ought to stake if off for them. I don't suppose you have a town site platted?"

"A town site? We're lucky to have a spring and a solid station house. I'll find something to mark corners," Mr. Joyton offered. "How big a place you goin' to build?"

"Just a small store in the front and living quarters in the rear."

"Do they want to stay in the barn?" Mr. Joyton asked.

"I have some used military tents in the store. I'll set up a string of them behind the store," Drakeville said.

The sun was straight up when Blaze brought Drew a cup of water. "You look like you need a drink. How's the work?"

"I got the hole dug, but I can't do anything else until Daddy has time to set those beams."

"I see you drug them over here."

Drew gulped down the water. It tasted cool and clean. "I didn't want them to become part of the new store."

She stared over his shoulder. "So you're making a headstone?"

"Well, a headboard."

"What did you put on it?"

"Take a look."

"'Unknown Man. Died of errant bullet. June 1, 1859.' I guess that says it all."

"With so many camped out around here, I figured we needed the marker up right away," Drew explained.

Blaze pointed across the dirt yard. "Is that an extra board?"

"Yep. There are several of these short ones."

"Paint us a Sonora Pass sign. We need a location sign besides the one on the store."

"What do you want it to say?"

"'Welcome to Sonora Pass, A.T."

"Sounds friendly."

"We are friendly."

"I figure a third of the population doesn't speak English, and another third is hidin' in a wagon and won't come out."

"And the other third are the delightful and friendly Joyton family," Blaze giggled.

"Do you reckon it's startin' to feel crowded around here?"

"It's probably only temporary. Daddy says with the Chiricahuas stirrin' up trouble, the more camped up here, the safer it is."

"What does Mama say?"

"She just sighs. You know Mama. She loves the wide-open spaces."

Drew surveyed the barren yard. "Do you know what we need? We need a flag."

"We don't have a flagpole," his sister pointed out.

"If we had a flag, maybe we'd get busy and find a flagpole."

"A cemetery, a store, a stage station, a flagpole, a swing, a sign—Drew Joyton, we almost have a town."

"Blaze, nobody would mistake Sonora Pass for a town."

"All towns begin somewhere."

"But towns have to have a reason to exist. Sonora Pass is just a stage stop. If the stage ever goes a different direction, there won't be any reason to be perched up here."

"I think the location's good. The Mexican trail comes in just east of here, the Sulphur Springs trail just west of us. Think of this as a commercial crossroad."

Drew gazed at the one building, one big tent, three little white tents, the tall adobe barn, corrals, and three cottonwood trees. "Commercial? More like comical," he hooted.

"Enough of that, Drew Joyton. Mark my words, I'm goin' to make a town of this place."

"Why?"

She wrinkled her nose. "It's either that, or I spend my days visiting with the chickens."

When Drew and Blaze entered the store, they both paused and stared.

"They have shelves!" he exclaimed.

Blaze shifted the hot apple pie from one hand to the other. "And merchandise in aisles."

"And crates open."

"And you can see everything," Blaze reported.

Naomi Drakeville stacked five-pound sacks of coarse salt on a crate near the front of the tent. "Sorry this is such a mess, but we'll have it straightened out by tomorrow. What with Mr. Drakeville and your papa laying out the store for the Mexicans, it leaves just the girls and me to tidy up."

"It looks wonderful, Mrs. Drakeville," Blaze assured her. "We just didn't know where to begin. . . . I baked you an apple pie."

Naomi Drakeville strolled over to them, her gray-black hair pulled tight behind her head. The lace collar of her black dress was stained with sweat. She took the pie and set it on the counter. "This is so nice of you. Natalie is our pie-baker, but we just got the cookstove hooked up about an hour ago."

"Have you run stores for a long time?" Drew asked.

"I've been working in stores since I was eight. My papa had a store in Arkansas. Actually in Arkansas, Texas, the Indian Nation, Louisiana, and Missouri. We traveled a lot."

"Daddy's always been a blacksmith and in the livery business," Drew explained. "But Mama needed the desert air for her cough."

"Did it help?" Mrs. Drakeville queried.

"Oh, yes. She's felt marvelous out here," Blaze responded.

"I'm hopin' it will do the same for me. Can I help you find anything, or are you just deliverin' this wonderful pie?"

"We came over to visit the girls," Blaze said. "Are they ready to receive company?"

"They're in back setting up house. Let me check."

"Setting up house?" Drew asked.

Mrs. Drakeville stood between Drew and Blaze. "Sorry to stare, honey, but you and your mother are about the tallest women I've ever been around. I suppose everyone says that."

"Yes, they do." Blaze nodded.

"And you're tired of people mentioning it?"

"No, not really," Blaze replied. "I do hate it when I get a compliment, as if I had something to do with it. The Lord creates us all just the way He chooses."

"I've been trying to get my girls to understand that. The good Lord don't make mistakes. We're all created in His image."

Drew glanced over at his sister. *Lord, I'm not sure what I'm getting into with this family. Help me to be kind and not stare or say anything dumb.*

"Stay here," Mrs. Drakeville said. "I'll check with the girls to see if they're presentable."

Blaze and Drew paused in front of a stack of gold pans.

"What do they need gold pans for around here?" Drew pondered.

"It was supposed to be sent to California, remember?" Blaze leaned a little closer. "Do you think there's something strange about these girls?" she whispered.

"I'm wonderin' if there's a reason they're hidin'."

"I'm trying to prepare myself to be gracious."

"I'm trying to prepare myself not to stare," Drew admitted.

"The youngest one, Nellie, looked normal enough when she stuck her head out of the wagon."

"We didn't see much of her but her smile. Blaze, you carry on the conversation. I don't talk well to girls."

"You talk to me all the time."

"That's different. You and me are pals."

"Think of them as pals. Maybe that will help."

Drew stared at the back of the tent. "Not if they look strange."

"We don't know that. Shhhh, here comes Mrs. Drakeville."

The short woman's heavy dark dress swished as she marched up to them. "You discussing our gold pans?"

"Yes, I'm sure they were meant for California. I don't know of too much placer mining around here," Drew said.

"Ah, that's the challenge to my Blair. He's a natural salesman."

"May we visit the girls now?" Blaze asked.

"Certainly. They're in their petticoats. So you'll have to stay on this side of the curtain. But there are some bolt kegs back there. You can use them for chairs."

Drew glanced over at Blaze, who was shaking her head. They strolled back to where a brand-new piece of canvas was stretched across the wall tent. Blaze sat on one wooden keg. Drew plopped down on the other.

Blaze cleared her throat. "Hi, girls, this is Blaze."

There was a chorus of giggles.

"Hi, this is Nancy. Is your brother with you?"

"Which one?"

"The one without the kite."

"The one with green eyes," another added.

"And strong shoulders," a third giggled.

Blaze reached over and patted his knee. "Yes, Drew is with me."

"How come he's not saying anything?"

"Eh, hi, girls," he choked.

"Hi, Drew."

"Hi, Drew."

"Hi, Drew. I won you."

"You—you what?"

"We drew straws, and I won you."

"It wasn't fair."

"It was too, wasn't it, Nellie?"

"Well, it was sorta fair."

Blaze leaned closer to the canvas. "Girls, from over here, we can't tell which one of you is speaking. Which one won Drew?"

"Me."

"But only for a week."

"We're goin' to draw straws again next week."

"But who won? Was it you, Natalie?"

"No, it was me—Nancy."

"When do we get to meet you face to face?" Blaze asked.

"When we're wearing more than a petticoat."

"What exactly does it mean that you won Drew?"

"It means that we can't drag him off to the barn," one of the girls giggled.

"Wha-at?" he stammered.

"I was just teasing."

"You were not."

"Well, I was sort of teasing."

"Girls, this is very confusing. Your voices sound alike," Blaze declared.

"You should hear us sing. We can harmonize quite well."

"Only one of us is slightly off key."

"I am not! It's papa's fiddle that's off."

"Who sings off key?" Blaze questioned.

"No one."

"She does too."

"They're jealous because I get more solos."

"You get solos because you're the only one in harmony with you."

Drew felt his head pound. *This is crazy. I don't even want to be here.*

"Hi, Mrs. Drakeville. Is my brother in there?" The voice started out high-pitched and changed mid-sentence.

Drew jumped up. "I'm back here, Talby. You need some help?"

"With what?" Talby called out.

"Eh, excuse me, girls. I have to help my brother."

"He didn't say that."

Talby wandered to the back of the store. "Who're you talkin' to?"

"The Drakeville girls," Blaze reported. "They're behind the curtain."

"Hi, Talby."

Talby jammed his hands in his back pockets. "Hi, Nellie. How's your arm?"

"Much better, thank you."

"Do you really need Drew to help you?"

"Not really, Nancy. I just wanted to tell him something."

"How did you know which one was talking?" Drew asked.

"They don't sound anything alike," Talby declared.

"Why did you come to fetch Drew?"

"I wanted to show him something, Natalie."

"I've got to go, girls," Drew insisted.

"Good-bye, sweetie."

"He's not your sweetie."

"He is for this week."

A red-faced Drew Joyton stomped out of the store.

"What's the matter with you . . . sweetie?" Talby chided.

"Which one called me sweetie?"

"That was Nancy. She's the oldest and tallest one."

"You mean, you've seen them?"

"I helped them move some boxes this morning."

"What do they look like?"

Talby shrugged. "Girls."

"What do you mean, girls?"

"You know—long hair, dresses, smooth complexion, giggles—they look like girls."

"I mean, are they, you know, handsome?"

"What do you mean, handsome?"

"Were they pretty?" Drew demanded.

"They were pretty short."

"All of them?"

"They're about the same height as Mrs. Drakeville."

"I can't believe you saw them and none of the rest of us have."

"I can't believe there's a hearse headed this way," Talby muttered.

"A what?"

"That's what I've been tryin' to tell you. I rode Snickers up to the pass, and there in the telescope I saw a hearse and several outriders comin' up the grade."

"Did you tell Mama?" Drew pressed.

"Yep, and Daddy too."

"How far away are they?"

Talby pointed up the road. "That's them right there."

Blaze scurried out of the tent and up to his side. "What's a hearse doin' here?"

"I reckon we'll find out," Drew murmured.

The first man down off the pass rode a gray mule right up to Blaze, Drew, and Talby. "Is there any whiskey in this town?" he blustered.

"Nope," Talby replied. "Ain't no saloon here."

Blaze poked Drew's side. "He called it a town. You said no one would call it a town."

"I reckon I was wrong," Drew admitted.

"Is there any medicinal wine?" the man pressed.

"Nope," Talby replied.

"Any rubbin' alcohol?"

"I'm afraid not," Blaze replied.

"Any spoiled cider?"

"No," Drew laughed. "You sound quite thirsty."

"Recovering bodies isn't my favorite thing to do. What in the world do you drink around here?"

"Coffee, tea, water, and cocoa," Blaze offered.

"Cocoa? This land is more primitive than I thought. Where's the coffee?"

"I'll show you." Blaze led the man toward the station house. "We do have some fresh apple pie."

"I reckon ever' place has its virtue," he mumbled.

The two men driving the hearse parked it by the cottonwoods just as Mr. Joyton came up.

"We got another customer for your cemetery," the driver called down.

"We don't really have a cemetery. It's just temporary," Mr. Joyton explained.

"We're all temporary on this earth. Some more temporary than others. We were told to bring his body to the cemetery at Sonora Pass."

"Who told you that?" Mr. Joyton queried.

"A man with a gray hat. He paid us good money to bring the body here. And there's five cash dollars for the burial plot and five for the gravedigger."

"Who's the dead man?" Drew asked.

"He fell out of the stagecoach. Said his name was Harold Weston, but ever'body calls him Pinch."

SIX

Talby ran across the road with a biscuit in his hand just as Drew finished brushing down St. Peter and ducked out the corral gate.

"Hey, where did the Mexicans go?" Talby called out.

"They went down to Cactus Flats. They said there was good clay down there; so that's where they will make the adobe blocks."

Talby stared north where the mountain dropped off to the desert floor. "I could have gone with them and flown my kite."

"Mr. Drakeville said they will be there until sunset."

"In that case, I'm glad I didn't go." Talby stuffed the biscuit into his mouth. "Kind of looks like a military camp around here, what with the big white tent and those three little ones the Mexicans have. I can almost hear a bugle call."

"Especially if we had a flag flyin'."

"Are we really goin' to run up a flag?" Talby asked.

"I've got the hole dug right over there by the wall. The Drakevilles have a flag. All we need is a pole."

"Are you goin' to get the swing up today?"

"I hope so, but we might have to wait until after the stage pulls in."

Talby wiped his mouth on the back of his hand. "Is it a Concord today?"

"I reckon it'll be a Celerity wagon. Whap said this route was too rough this time of the year for the Concords. They're only goin' to use them for special passengers."

"Have you seen if the Drakeville girls are up yet?" Talby asked.

"I've never seen the Drakeville girls," Drew replied.

"I'll go check. I promised Nellie I'd show her how far we can see with my telescope."

"You're goin' to go visit with Nellie?"

"Yeah."

"Face to face?"

"Sure, what's wrong with that?"

"Not a thing, little brother."

"Did you know she is six months, fourteen days, and ten hours older than me?" Talby said.

"No, I don't reckon I knew that."

"I told her that's okay 'cause I like older girls."

"You do?" Drew laughed.

"Sure, Mama and Blaze are older than me too."

"Are you and Nellie goin' to go somewhere and look through the telescope?"

"That's a grand idea. Maybe we can ride down to Cactus Flats. I'll show her how to fly a kite horseback."

"I think they'll want you to stay closer to home. You could take her up on the roof."

"Nah, she's scared of heights. One time she fell out of a barn and busted her arm, and now she won't even climb two steps on a ladder. They had a two-story house in Missouri, but she took the bedroom downstairs."

Drew meandered with his brother toward the store. "How did you find out all of that?"

"She told me."

"What does Nancy look like?" Drew asked.

"I told you. She looks sort of like Blaze."

"Really?"

"Except she's short, doesn't have red hair, and has brown eyes."

"Then she doesn't look anything like Blaze."

"I wasn't just talkin' about her face." Talby scooted toward the store. "I think we'll hike up to the top of the pass and look west in the telescope."

When Drew and his father had readied the relay horses, they hiked across the road to the house. Within half an hour they had set the end post for the swing, augured holes in the roof joist, and bolted on the crossbeam. Drew held the ladder while Rand Joyton wrenched down the eyebolts he had forged. Two ropes hung straight down when Drew returned with the wooden swing seat he had made.

"Where's little brother goin' with Miss Drakeville?" his father asked.

Drew looked up the road. Talby and a short girl in blue gingham hiked toward the pass. She wore a matching bonnet.

"I think he wants to show her his telescope."

"He's quite friendly with the girls." Mr. Joyton grinned.

"Yeah, and they won't even meet me face to face."

"Which one is he with?"

"The youngest one, Nellie."

Mr. Joyton threaded the rope through the swing seat and tied if off underneath. "Time for you to try it out."

"No, I promised Blaze the first swing. I'll be right back."

He stooped through the doorway and entered the big room. His sister sat by the window, combing her damp red hair.

"It's ready for you, sis."

She laid down the brush. "The swing?"

"Yep, me and Daddy got it done."

Blaze jumped up. "Mama, the swing's done. Come on!"

Mrs. Joyton wiped her hands on her white apron. "I haven't even set my hair up yet."

Blaze grabbed her hand. "Come on, Mama!" They both ducked under the doorway and out into the yard.

"Oh, yes," Blaze giggled. She scampered around and sat facing the north with a panoramic view of the desert floor far below. Then she grabbed the ropes, ran back, jumped on the seat, and swung forward.

"Push me, Drew," she hollered. "Push me higher. Oh, it's so wonderful!"

After a few minutes, Blaze hopped out. "It's your turn, Mama."

"Oh, no, let Drew go ahead."

"No, Mama," he insisted. "Ladies first."

"All right, I'll just do that." She marched over and plopped down into the swing.

"Push me, Rand."

Mr. Joyton gave his wife a shove.

"Higher," she shouted.

"That's gettin' pretty high now, darlin'."

"Higher!" Ceva Joyton demanded.

Soon she was swinging out over the low adobe wall. "Stand back, everyone," she called out.

"What're you goin' to do?" Drew questioned.

"I'm goin' to fly!" Mrs. Joyton shouted.

She laid her head back so far that her hair almost dragged on the dirt. She held her legs straight out in front and dove for the dirt every time the swing came back.

"My word, Ceva," Mr. Joyton called out, "your skirt is billowing in the wind."

"Yes," she laughed. "And it truly does feel wonderful!"

Only a holler from the top of the pass stopped the swing. "Is Talby in trouble?" Mrs. Joyton asked.

Drew ran out to the road. Talby and Nellie trotted down the grade. A bonnet shaded her face. "Daddy, the stage is at Deception Rock, and I spotted that boy, Tease Banyon, hiking up the west grade near Faraway Perch," Talby shouted.

Mr. Joyton jogged out to the road. "Banyon is on foot?"

"Yep, and he looks tuckered out."

"Drew, harness up a team to the wagon. Go fetch Tease. I need to stay here for the stage. Talby, you help me switch teams."

Mrs. Joyton leaped out of the swing and scooted toward the front door. "I'll go warm up dinner."

Nellie looked up. Drew was caught by her smooth, pale face and bright blue eyes. Brown curls framed her face. "Can I help, Mrs. Joyton?" she asked.

"Mama, let Nellie serve coffee. I'll go with Drew," Blaze offered.

Mrs. Joyton paused and glanced at Rand. He nodded. "If young Banyon is on foot, there's some trouble. Drew, you and sis take St. Peter and St. Paul and your shotgun."

By the time Drew drove the wagon up the pass, the stage had pulled into the station. He glanced over his shoulder and could see Talby run another team up to his father.

"Little brother is doin' okay," he murmured.

"He just needs a chance to work. Speaking of little brother, that Nellie Drakeville is a cutie," Blaze offered.

"Did you see her—"

"Blue eyes? Oh, my, you can see those a mile away."

"She'd be even cuter without the bonnet," Drew mumbled.

"By all means, I'll recommend she keeps it on." Blaze grinned. "The Joyton boys will be fighting over her as it is."

"No, we won't."

"Oh, that's right—it was Nancy that won you."

Drew sighed, shook his head, and slapped the lead lines again. He brought the wagon to a stop at the top of Sonora Pass. They surveyed the western slope.

"Do you see him?" Blaze asked.

"No, maybe he's down on one of the switchbacks."

Blaze clutched the shotgun at the sound of a howl. "Did you hear that?"

"Yeah, they're out there."

"Do you want the shotgun, Drew, and let me drive?"

"No, I'm a better driver, and you're a better shot. Let's get him and get out of here." Drew slapped the lead lines. The team bolted down the grade toward the distant desert floor.

Hooves pounded.

Axles squeaked.

The wagon rattled.

Blaze clutched the long-barreled shotgun with one hand and Drew's arm with the other as dust fogged around them.

Drew reined up at Faraway Perch. "Where is he?"

The wolf howl came from about fifty feet south of the wagon.

"They're close, Drew!" Blaze stood and pointed the shotgun to the south.

Drew stood up and shouted, "Tease! Socrates Banyon . . . this is Drew and Blaze. Where are you? Hurry! They're movin' in!"

A boulder the size of a large watermelon rolled down the hill, and Tease Banyon crawled out of the rocks. His clothes were torn. He was covered with dirt. "There was too many of them. My pistol is empty. I had to hide."

"Get in the wagon," Drew shouted.

"Possum got shot in the head. I think he's dead," Tease hollered.

"Run, Tease, run!" Blaze shouted.

Banyon sprinted and dove in the back of the wagon just as Drew whipped the lines and circled the wagon to the south. They bounced along the desert and got back on the road. Drew slapped the lines, and St. Peter and St. Paul galloped up to the pass.

"Where're you goin'?" Tease shouted.

"To the station," Drew replied.

"We got to go get Zink. He's shot in the leg," Tease screamed.

"Where is he?" Blaze asked.

"At Rotten Egg Gulch."

"That's too far, Tease. That's over ten miles. We can't go without help," Drew declared.

Socrates Banyon's voice broke with panic. "No, we have to get back to Zink. I promised."

Drew continued to race the wagon up the mountain.

Tease grabbed Drew's arm and tried to latch onto the lines. Drew shoved him back. Banyon tripped and fell back in the wagon.

"You don't understand. They'll kill him," Banyon shouted.

"And you don't understand. They'll kill all of us tryin' to get to him. We have to get more help," Drew shot back.

"No," Banyon screamed. "We have to get Zink and Possum." He lunged again at Drew, but this time Blaze shoved the shotgun in his chest. He staggered to the back of the wagon. She held her finger on the trigger.

"Surely, you won't shoot me," he yelled.

"Don't ever, ever underestimate what I would do to protect my brother," Blaze barked. "Now sit down and don't move until we get to the station."

Socrates Banyon flopped down in the wagon, fear and frustration in his face.

When they crested the pass, Blaze spun around and sat down next to Drew.

"Thanks, sis. He don't mean it. He's scared."

"I know. But I meant it," she said.

"Yep. I know you do. And so does Socrates Banyon—now."

When they thundered into the station, Rand Joyton, Blair Drakeville, and the stage driver, Royce Purline, were waiting for them. It took several minutes to get Tease

Banyon coherent enough to describe what happened. Then Blaze and Talby took him to the kitchen to get something to eat.

"I've got to go on, Joyton," Purline declared. "Butterfield's got a big contract with the government to deliver the mail. I can't slow down. We can make it. Cole's ridin' shotgun, and once we get beyond Faraway Perch, we give 'em line and let 'em run all the way to Hart Station."

"You goin' to give the passengers a choice?" Mr. Joyton asked.

"Can you put 'em up if they want to stay?"

"You know we can."

"Then I'll tell them," Purline announced.

"Get word to the army what's happenin' here," Rand Joyton requested.

"I'll do that." Purline hiked into the stage station.

Within moments, he and Cole Fleck trotted out to the stage. Three men and two women scurried out behind them.

"Are they all goin'?" Drew asked.

"No, they're all stayin'. I told them to get their satchels and personals," Purline explained.

Ceva Joyton jogged out with a grub sack just as they were ready to pull out. "Take some biscuits and salt pork. You didn't get to finish your lunch." She tossed it up to Cole Fleck.

"Thank you, Mrs. Joyton. Pray for us," Cole said.

"I always do," she replied. "All you drivers know that."

The stage left a cloud of dust.

And worried passengers.

"Joyton, you think them savages will station?" one asked.

"The Chiricahuas will do what they fi to do. And we'll do the same. I would rather side get killed, but we'll defend the station." He pointed toward the barn. "Drew, you got a saddle on Carlos?"

"Yep."

Rand Joyton turned to the shopkeeper. "Blair, you're the only one who speaks Spanish. Ride down to Cactus Flats and call your crew of Mexicans back up here. It's too dangerous for them down there. If they get attacked, we can't leave our position up here and go help them."

"What about Zink and Possum?" Drew asked.

"Where's Tease?"

"Blaze has him occupied."

"Oh?"

"She's makin' him wash up and eat a little food. But don't worry, she's still totin' the shotgun, Daddy."

Rand Joyton rubbed his clean-shaven chin. "We can go get them if we take four mules and six armed men in a wagon. Chances are, there aren't more than a dozen warriors. They won't attack half a dozen guns, especially in a wagon that keeps movin'."

"Why four mules? Don't that slow you down?" one of the passengers asked.

"We can lose a couple and still make it back."

A man in a suit and tie stepped up. "You aren't expectin' us to go with you, are you?"

Rand stared at the three men. "No . . . I reckon not. I need men with courage and sand."

"That ain't fair, Joyton. We don't figure to take risks for men we don't even know."

"I suppose that's the difference between you and me."

Blaze and Tease Banyon scrambled out to the others. Mrs. Drakeville crossed the road just as her husband galloped east on Carlos.

"Even if we went, there's only three of us," one of the passengers pointed out. "That makes four guns at best 'cause you sent the storekeeper down to fetch the Mexicans."

"We have enough guns," Blaze declared.

Ceva pulled off her apron and handed it to one of the male passengers. "There're dishes in there to do. I'll expect them done by the time we get back."

"You're goin' with him?" the man gasped.

"I'll go and protect my man any day. Besides, I can outshoot him."

"I'm goin' too. I need to protect Drew and Talby," Blaze declared.

"You can't risk your whole family for two men as good as dead," a passenger protested.

"Mister, I can't do anything else. Jesus risked it all for you and me."

"Yeah, and He was crucified," the man blustered.

Ceva Joyton folded her arms across her chest. "At last look, the tomb was empty."

"Drew and I will hitch the mules to the wagon. You gals get the gunpowder and shot," Mr. Joyton commanded. "Mrs. Drakeville, as soon as your husband gets back, have him determine how to protect this place. Chances are they won't come in here until after dark, if they come at all. We'll be back in four or five hours. If there are any others on the road, tell them to wait here at the station."

The mules bolted up the hill the moment the lines

slapped against their rumps. Ceva Joyton sat on the seat beside Rand, the .52-caliber Sharps across her lap. Behind her Talby was on his knees, the navy revolver in his hand. Tease Banyon sat behind Mr. Joyton. Blaze and Drew faced the tailgate. She toted the shotgun; he held the .45-caliber revolver.

The long red hair of both women flagged bonnetless in the wind.

"I can't believe the whole family is goin'," Tease said as the wagon crested the pass and veered south on the trail to Sulphur Springs.

"Didn't have much choice," Mr. Joyton said.

"Besides, we have to take care of each other. That's why the Lord put us here on earth," Ceva Joyton explained.

"You people believe in Jesus?"

"He's our Lord and Savior, Tease," Ceva declared. "We take it all very serious."

"I did some serious praying when I was tryin' to outrun the Apaches through the desert."

"What did you pray?" Mrs. Joyton pressed.

"I told God if He would deliver me, I'd believe He's real, and I'd be willin' to say so to any who wanted to know."

"Is he real to you now?" Mrs. Joyton asked.

"The day ain't over yet, but there has to be somethin' that made all of you do this."

The hooves thundered. The wagon squeaked. But the wolves didn't howl this time. There was no sign of movement on the desert.

"Daddy, do you think we outran them?" Drew hollered.

"They can't be stretched all along the road to Sulphur Springs. There just aren't that many of them. If they were back there by the road, they can't be out here."

"Some of them are still back at Rotten Egg Gulch," Tease reminded him.

The sun was halfway down the western horizon as they approached the rim of Rotten Egg Gulch. For a few days during the year, it was a creek.

This was not one of those days.

Mr. Joyton hollered back, "Where are they, Tease?"

"In a cave down at that bend."

"We can't get down in that sand and risk getting the wagon stuck. And we can't stop, or the Apaches will bunch up on us. If we keep movin', we'll keep them spread out. We've got to get the freighters to the rim up here."

"Possum's dead. He'll be too heavy to carry," Tease objected.

"Then who's that wavin' at us?" Mrs. Joyton pointed to the dry, sandy creek bed.

"That's . . . that's Possum!" Tease hollered. "What's he doin' alive?"

"Tryin' to signal us, it looks like. Tease, you and Drew dive off the wagon when I slow down," Mr. Joyton ordered. "You bring them over to the rim. I'll circle out on the desert and draw the Indians away from the gulch. Then we'll swing back and pick you all up."

"Are you kiddin' me?" Tease gasped.

"How much time do we have?" Drew hollered.

"Sing 'Amazing Grace,' and I'll be back." Rand Joyton slowed the wagon down near the rim of the dry creek bed.

"I'm not jumpin' down there," Tease gulped.

"How many verses, Daddy?" Blaze called out.

"Four."

"Come on, Drew." Blaze grabbed her brother's hand. They leaped off the back of the wagon and ran down to the sandy creek bed.

Blaze toted the shotgun and sang, "'Amazing grace, how sweet the sound . . .'"

They dashed toward the cave where Possum Summerfield crouched behind a boulder.

"'. . . that saved a wretch like me,'" Blaze continued.

"Come on," Drew shouted. "Daddy's circlin' out and comin' back for us."

"Zink's been leg-shot."

Blaze pointed to Possum's bloody bandanna. "And you were shot in the head."

"Lucky for me they didn't hit no vital organ."

"'I once was lost and now am found,'" Blaze continued.

"You grab one shoulder," Drew called out to Possum. "I'll get the other. Blaze will cover us."

With gun at her shoulder and red hair flowing down, Blaze led the trio up the sandy draw. "'. . . was blind but now I see.'"

SEVEN

I'm gassed. I can't make it," Zink Chadron puffed. His entire 180-pound, sweaty, unbathed frame hung from the shoulders of Drew and Possum Summerfield.

Blaze stiffened her shoulders and kept hiking through the hot, dry creek bed. "'Twas grace that taught my heart to fear, and grace my fears relieved,'" she sang just above a whisper.

Drew's knees burned. His side cramped. The air he gulped in tasted used, almost dead. "Come on, Mr. Chadron . . . you can do it," he urged.

With green eyes wide, Blaze searched the sagebrush that huddled on the rim. "'How precious did that grace appear the hour I first believed.'"

"My leg is dead, son," Zink insisted. "You all have to go on. Save yourselves. Jist leave me a gun and a bullet."

Possum staggered in the sand, and Blaze took his place to drag the injured freighter. "'The Lord has promised good to me, His word my hope secures,'" she sang, her voice raspy.

"Mr. Chadron, we're takin' you with us; so no more talk like that." Drew's salty sweat dripped off his forehead to his lips. "You're too tough an old teamster to lay down in the sand and die. Isn't that right, Possum?"

"The boy's right, Zink. We've got more loads to haul." Possum glanced over his shoulder as he hurried to catch up with the others. "A couple of them is comin' up the riverbed behind us," he shouted.

They paused out in the open sand.

Drew craned his head "Where?" *Be near to us, Lord. We surely need Your protection.*

"On the south bank," Possum hollered.

Drew studied the sage and spotted long black hair and buckskin trousers. "Let them know we see them, sis," Drew said.

Blaze threw the shotgun to her shoulder and spun around. "'He will my shield and portion be, as long as life endures.'" She pulled the trigger. The gun roared flame and thick gray smoke.

"You cain't hit them with a scattergun this far away." Zink tossed his arm around the tall girl's shoulder.

Drew staggered forward. "No, but she can let them know we have our eye on them. Now come on . . . get ready to climb this bank."

"We can't go up there. What if they're waitin' for us?" Possum Summerfield protested.

Blaze stood tall, shoulders back, red hair flowing to her waist. "'When we've been there ten thousand years, bright shining as the sun . . .'"

Possum Summerfield dragged the butt stock of his breech-loader in the sand. "I don't see the wagon. Where's your daddy?"

"He'll be there the minute we get up out of here," Drew insisted.

Possum stared behind them. "How can you be so sure?"

"'Cause Blaze is singin' the fourth verse."

They had just shoved Zink Chadron to the top of the riverbank when the wagon rumbled up. Hot sand and dirt trickled between Drew's fingers as he pulled himself up on the rim. He whipped around and offered his hand to his sister, his eyes searching the creek bed behind them. He yanked her up. Together they pulled up Possum Summerfield.

"'We've no less days to sing God's praise than when we'd first begun,'" Blaze finished.

Mr. Joyton shoved the lead lines at his wife and jumped down. In less than a minute they had everyone loaded in the wagon. Zink and Possum huddled in the middle with the Joyton family around the outside. The four mules strained at the harness and galloped north with muted hooves across the roadless desert.

"You got us some help, Socrates Banyon. I'm proud of ya, boy," Possum blurted out. The bandanna around his head was striped blood-red.

Tease rubbed dirt off the back of his neck, his face drawn tight about wild brown eyes. "But I didn't dive off in the sand like Drew and Blaze."

"That's all right, boy. You hiked back through them savages and got us help," Zink added. "Ain't one man in a hundred could have done that." He ripped his ducking trousers back. The broken shaft of an arrow poked out from the bloody leg wound.

Drew turned away and watched the desert floor as the wagon raced north.

Tease scooted back by Blaze and Drew. "Are they still out there?"

"I reckon so," Drew said.

"I don't see them."

"You never see Apaches unless they want you to see them."

"Will they try to stop the wagon?"

"I don't think so. I haven't seen any horses. And if they're all on foot, they won't get in front of those four mules. Even Daddy wouldn't slow down then."

"They could block the road," Tease said.

"There isn't any road," Blaze pointed out. "And they don't know which path we'll take. That's why Daddy isn't driving in a straight line."

For an hour the wagon rattled, and no one spoke. Drew peered over his shoulder from time to time to watch Zink Chadron chew on his leather suspenders as he dug the obsidian arrowhead out of his leg with a boot knife's twelve-inch blade.

Blaze sat with her head down to her knees. Drew studied the empty desert and dusty trail. *Lord, I don't know how anyone can do surgery on themselves like that. Zink's got to be one of the toughest men I ever met in my life. Yet he needed me and Blaze to bring him out of the creek bed. I reckon we all have different things to do in this life.*

Zink Chadron tossed the arrowhead to the wagon floor and wrapped the wound with a bloody flour sack. Then he broke the silence. "Missy, when I first heard you singing, I thought it was angels. I surely did."

Blaze sat up. "I would imagine angels sing much better than that."

Chadron picked up the arrowhead and ran his thumb across it. "They might, missy, but I doubt if I ever hear any tune that sounds sweeter. My mama used to sing 'Amazing Grace' all the time. She was singing it when she died."

"I thought I might be doing the same thing," Blaze said. "I suppose it's as good a last song as any."

"You should have seen that sight," Possum added. "Your brother there with his strong, wide shoulders, and you with that flowin' red hair—both of you as tall as Goliath—marchin' right down the middle of that creek bed. It was a picture of biblical proportions, all right. It was like divine deliverance."

Ceva Joyton leaned back. "Possum, give the Lord the credit if we make it back safe to the station. It *was* divine deliverance. We get no credit for doing what we are told."

Zink studied his wound. "Mrs. Joyton, I reckon I will have a lot to be thankful for if I survive all of this. I won't ever forget when a whole family saved me from certain death."

No one relaxed until they came to the stage road and turned east up the mountain.

Tease stared down at his boots and mumbled, "I was too scared to jump off the wagon. I don't how you two did it."

Drew rolled his eyes at Blaze. "We didn't think about it much, did we, sis?"

She pulled a linen handkerchief from her sleeve and wiped a smudge off Drew's cheek. "We did it together. Sometimes it's easier if you take a leap with someone else. Drew and I have been partners in adventures for years."

Tease rubbed his chin and left finger lines across his cheek. "I planned on bein' brave; then I couldn't do it."

"I don't know if anyone can plan on bein' brave," Drew commented. "'Cause what you think you'll do never has the same feelin' as actually havin' to do it."

"I think maybe we did this whole trip without thinkin' too much," Blaze admitted.

"But we surely were trusting the Lord," Talby called out.

"I reckon that's where you got me beat," Tease replied. "I ain't never had to trust Him before."

"Sure you have," Blaze countered.

"What do you mean?" Tease questioned.

"When you went to sleep last night, did you expect the sun to come up today?" Blaze asked.

"Yeah, I reckon."

"When you ate supper, did you expect it to bring nourishment?" Drew quizzed.

"We didn't have any supper last night. We was hidin' from Apaches. But I know what you're sayin'."

"Faith is believing everything the Lord tells us and acting on that belief," Blaze explained.

"I always figured that faith was a bunch of things you think about in your head," Socrates Banyon remarked.

"That's only part of it," Blaze told him.

"Weren't you scared when you jumped out?"

Drew scratched the back of his neck. "When we left the wagon, I thought I would throw up. My stomach was churnin' so . . . but when I heard Blaze singin', I got too busy tryin' to get to Zink and Possum to be afraid."

"Why did you sing?"

"Because of the timing of the song," Blaze explained. "But also because I was so scared my lips would start to quiver if I didn't."

"When Blaze's lips quiver, her hands and her knees start shaking too," Drew said.

Tease shook his head. "I can't believe you'd do that when you were scared."

"Part of it's that we couldn't live with ourselves if we didn't," Drew admitted. "After drivin' two hours to find them, we couldn't go off and leave them there in the creek bed."

"I surely felt foolish hunkerin' in the back of the wagon and you two runnin' down that creek bed," Tease muttered.

"Your part was to hike back and get help," Drew said. "Our part was to pull them out of the creek bed. We just had to do our parts—that's all."

Mr. Joyton didn't slow the wagon until it crested the pass and the station was in view. With the sun low in the sky, the stage stop was flooded by evening shadows.

"Looks like we have more company," Talby shouted.

"Blaze, we'll have a lot of cooking tonight," Mrs. Joyton called back. "I'll need your help."

"Someone has to doctor Mr. Chadron's leg," Drew said.

"I just need to clean this wound and sew it up. I'll be okay," Zink declared. "I've been hurt worse than this when a grizzly bear crawled into our tent."

"There are freight wagons full of logs blockin' the road," Talby hollered. "Look, there are six small tents now. We look like a fort. Fort Sonora."

When they rolled up to the station, they were greeted by a dozen people.

Drew unhitched the mules and rubbed them down.

He had just put the last one up when Talby scurried out to him.

"Sergeant Thorton said he would give us his puniest log for a flagpole."

"Where is he headed with his men?" Drew asked.

"To Fort Aravaipa."

"How many soldiers are with him?"

"Just one and the two teamsters driving the wagons," Talby reported. "The troops are circling the Dragoon Mountains. There are reports of the Chiricahua Apache causin' trouble down there."

"They're up here now. But it's great to get a flagpole."

Mr. Drakeville and the Mexicans ate supper first and then stood guard behind the wagons loaded with logs as the others filed into the dining room.

Mrs. Drakeville cleaned Zink Chadron's wound with horse liniment, then sewed up his wound and duckings. She took supper to Nancy and Natalie at the store. Nellie Drakeville assisted Blaze. Ceva Joyton served the guests. After all were seated and grace was said, Rand Joyton addressed the crowd.

"Folks, we don't have any idea of the intentions of the band of Apaches in this area. But we're goin' to be prepared. We'll keep four men on guard, and I'll be with the horses in the corral. The women passengers will stay in the station. The men will share the tents. Sergeant Thorton is in charge of rotating the night guard."

The heaviest of the women brushed down her navy serge suit and patted her forehead with a napkin. "Which of the men will be on guard at our front door?"

Mr. Joyton nodded across the room. "My daughter Blaze will do that."

"I'd feel much safer with a man there," the large woman huffed.

"I wouldn't," Possum Summerfield responded. "That gal and her brother put their lives on the line for me and Zink. None of the rest of you proved you had that much courage."

"They can stand guard over me any night of the year," Zink added. "And I'll sleep like a baby."

The woman cleared her throat. "I, eh, I suppose with those recommendations, it would be acceptable."

Rand Joyton continued, "I'm not sayin' this to alarm anyone, but I'd suggest we sleep fully dressed. We might have to react rapidly."

"Sergeant Thorton, I demand to know when the troops will be here to escort us on to Tucson," one of the male passengers insisted. "I have no intention of staying at this godforsaken place one moment longer than absolutely necessary. We were promised military escort at El Paso."

The sergeant broke open a steaming biscuit and smeared it with butter. "Mister, you knew the risks when you came west. We'll do what we deem best to protect the most number of people with the few troops that we have. And I can assure you, as long as the Joyton family is here, God has not forsaken Sonora Pass."

"When do you expect the troops to return?" another woman asked.

"If they find no resistance, they'll be at Sulphur Springs tonight and circle around from the west tomorrow."

It was almost dark when Drew and Mr. Joyton moved the milk cows inside the low adobe wall. All of the horses were tied to a rope picket line outside the wall. The mules were crowded into the barn. The corrals stood empty.

"It looks like an army camp for sure now, with the horses all lined up like this," Drew observed.

"They'll have to get by our defenses before they get to the horses. The corrals are too exposed," his father explained.

"Daddy, can we raise the flagpole?" Drew asked.

"It's gettin' late, son. We'll do it tomorrow."

"But tomorrow will be hectic. It's a big pole. I'd like to do it while we have help."

Mr. Joyton studied the camp. "You might be right."

Blaze and Nellie meandered out into the yard.

"Ain't no one for miles," Talby shouted from the roof where he stood twilight guard with his telescope. "At least, no one out in the open."

"We're goin' to raise the flagpole," Drew told the girls.

"I'll go get Daddy's flag," Nellie offered.

"I'll bolt on the eye hook," Rand Joyton said. "Drew, go get Sergeant Thorton and the teamsters. They're in those last two tents."

It took the combined effort of six men to lift the twenty-four-foot pole and slide it down into Drew's hole. He and Mr. Joyton packed fist-sized rocks around the pole's buried base and tamped in reddish yellow dirt.

Blaze and Nellie Drakeville circled camp, informing them all of the flag-raising ceremony. By the time they gathered, it was almost dark. Nancy and Natalie came out of the store for the first time, but with both wearing bonnets, Drew couldn't see either of their faces.

Ceva Joyton carried out the biggest lantern.

"My word," one of the stage passengers complained, "dare we offer an illuminated target?"

"What's the point of raising a flag if we can't see it?" Ceva turned to the only man in uniform. "Sergeant Thorton, would the army mind if for one night we left our flag up instead of lowering it? It's a symbol that brings some measure of confidence to my heart."

"We can do that," the sergeant said. "This is not a military camp. You folks don't have to follow military rules. Do you want Pencil O'Brien to play his bugle?"

"Oh, yes." Blaze clapped her hands. "Play the bugle as we raise the flag."

"We don't want to broadcast our location," the big woman in the navy serge gasped.

The sergeant laughed. "I can assure you, ma'am, they already know where we are. Secrecy is not an option we have been allowed."

"Who's goin' to raise the flag?" O'Brien asked, bugle in hand.

"Drew dug the hole and pushed us to get a flag up," Mr. Joyton said. "I suggest he do it."

"Blaze can help me. We sort of thought of it together."

With the big lantern at the base of the tall flagpole, the flag was illuminated as the stars blinked on in the black Arizona night. Mr. Drakeville helped them tie the flag in place and then nodded at O'Brien. The bugler blew reverie. Hand over fist, Drew and Blaze raised the flag. The sergeant stood at attention, the others with hands over their hearts.

A cool desert breeze caught the flag and trailed it out to the east as it neared the top of the pole. The crowd remained quiet until O'Brien finished.

"Mama, can we leave the light here for a while? It casts a nice light on the flag," Talby asked.

"And it gives a point of reference no matter where anyone is in camp," Drew added.

"Is that acceptable, Sergeant?" Mrs. Joyton asked.

"Until someone takes a shot at us. Then the light goes out," he declared.

Drew sat cross-legged under the buckboard, the shotgun across his lap, staring into the dark mountain south of Sonora Pass Station. He heard someone approach behind him.

"Hi, sis," he murmured.

"You always know when it's me."

"Yep."

She crawled under the wagon. "Have you seen anything?"

"Nothin' besides Venus, Capella, and Polaris."

"Did Daddy want to leave the team hitched to the wagon?"

"Yep, we saddled all the horses we could and got the wagons hitched just in case we need to make a run for it," Drew explained.

"We've been here for a year without a serious Indian attack. Why are we so worried about this one?" Blaze asked.

"Maybe 'cause we have more folks to worry about."

"I don't think they'll attack this big a settlement."

"We'll find out."

"If they attack, it'll be right before dawn, I would imagine."

"That's what I'm thinkin'," Drew said.

"Is Daddy out there in the empty corral?"

"Or prowlin' around in front of it. He wants to be the first in line."

"He hasn't slept very much in two or three nights. Mama said she was worried about him."

"Have you ever known Daddy to let this family down?"

"No, you're right, Drew. If Daddy didn't want me at the door to the station, I'd stay out here with you. Is Talby out here?" she asked.

"He said he was stayin' on the roof."

"He can't see anything at night."

"He said he would study Andromeda if there was nothin' else to look at."

"You know what I was thinking, Drew?"

"What?"

"I was thinkin' about Esther in the Bible."

"You mean . . . that we are 'come to the kingdom for such a time as this?'"

"Yes. Do you suppose we've been living out here just for a time like these past few days?"

"I've been wonderin' that too. I still can't believe that you and me dove off that wagon, Blaze. I would never have done it without you grabbin' my hand."

"Dear brother, don't you ever think I could do that without you. I probably would have hunkered down like Tease."

"He's okay, sis. He made it to the road on foot and alone with Chiricahuas all around. I don't think I could do that."

"I think he's matured a little in the past few days."

"Tonight might just mature us all."

"I guess I'll get back to guardin' the front door and the womenfolk." Blaze spoke in a fake low voice.

"Take care of yourself, sis."

She crawled out from under the wagon, then squatted down. "Drew, if we have to pull out in a hurry, let's you and me go together, okay?"

"I won't leave without you."

"Thanks."

Drew watched his sister stroll past the lantern at the base of the flagpole and fade into the shadows of the front yard. *Lord, I've known boys that hated their sisters. But Blaze is my very best friend. I surely like it that way.*

The receiver on his shotgun was cold in his hand. His eyelids were sagging when he heard footsteps behind him again.

It sounded like a girl's dress swishing.

But not Blaze's.

"Drew, is that you under the wagon?"

With the faint lantern behind her, all he could see was a silhouette, a girl in a long dress and bonnet. "Nellie, is that you?"

"It's, uh . . . Nancy."

He scooted out from under the wagon and stood. Drew held his shotgun in one hand and his hat in the other. "Howdy, Nancy. What're you doin' out in the dark?"

"What're you doing?"

"I'm takin' my turn at guard. Me and Daddy are the southern guard."

"Drew, do you really think the Apaches will attack?"

"Not until it's close to daylight. They know we have guns."

"Can I sit out here awhile?" she asked.

"Eh, sure . . . but I don't have a blanket."

"What is that supposed to mean?"

"I mean, you don't want to sit in the dirt, do you?"

She sat down right where she stood. "Why not?"

Drew sat down next to her. "Can I ask you a question, Nancy?"

"All right."

"How come you've never come out to talk to me face to face?"

"I'm here now."

"Yeah, but . . . but I can't see your face."

"And I can't see yours. What difference does that make?"

"Sooner or later can I see you?"

"Why? Do you want to be my beau? Just because I won you doesn't mean you're my beau."

"What?" Drew choked. "I mean—I . . ."

"Oh my, you do stammer easily."

"Can we change the subject?"

"Certainly. What do you want to talk about?"

"Eh . . . how about, eh . . . stars . . . night sky."

Her voice was soft. Sweet. Almost a song. Almost a whisper. "Is that Vega over there in the west, Drew?"

Drew was back under the wagon when Talby scooted in next to him. "It ain't very heroic sittin' up on the roof."

"Maybe you should slip into the house and get some sleep."

"I ain't turnin' tail."

"You plannin' on guardin' the Drakevilles?"

"Which one came to visit you?" Talby asked.

"Nancy."

"She's purdy, ain't she? Did you see them dimples?"

"She was easy to talk to, but I didn't see her face."

"She's surely purdy. I'm goin' to find me some jerky. You want me to bring you some?"

"Sure."

"I don't reckon that's heroic either," Talby mumbled.

Talby hadn't been gone two minutes before Drew heard more footsteps.

"Drew?"

"Tease?"

"Yeah. How's it goin'?"

"Kind of boring so far," Drew admitted.

Tease crawled under the wagon. "I couldn't sleep. I got a question for you."

"What's that?"

"Do you think your God will accept just anybody?"

"Nope," Drew replied.

"I didn't think so either."

"He only accepts sinners," Drew said.

"Really? I thought it was just the opposite."

Drew never took his eyes off the blackness to the south. "Those who think they're okay don't need help, do they?"

"I reckon not. So if He only takes sinners," Tease murmured, "there's a chance for me?"

"Yep."

Tease visited until Mr. Joyton refilled the oil in the flagpole lantern, checked all the horses, and then hiked out to the edge of the empty corral.

Footsteps again caused Drew to lean back in the dirt and peer out.

"Drew?" a girl whispered.

"Hi, I'm down here. Who is it?"

"It's me—Nancy."

"What happened to your voice?" Drew asked.

"What do you mean?"

"You sound different."

"Different than what?"

"Than you did earlier."

"Earlier? I didn't come out here earlier."

"Of course you did. We sat here talkin' about the stars and the desert and, you know . . . stuff."

"What kind of stuff?" she pressed.

"You know."

"Did Natalie come out here and pretend to be me?"

"I don't know. Was it her?"

"Of course it was. We don't look anything alike."

Drew glanced up into the dark silhouette of the girl in the long dress and bonnet. He closed his eyes, then opened them wide. *Maybe I'm just dreaming all of this.*

EIGHT

Something thick hung in the air when Drew sat up.

He heard nothing.

He saw nothing.

But he could feel it.

They're out there. They're all over. They're very, very close. Where's my shotgun? I can't find my shotgun.

Drew patted the dirt under the wagon. He swung his arms around. His hands clutched something soft.

A loaf of bread?

Where did the bread come from?

I'm about to get scalped, and all I have is a loaf of bread?

He swung the bread around in the dark in front of him like a sword. He heard footsteps. He tried to shout. Nothing came out.

What am I going to do? I can't even warn the others. I'm too scared to sound the alarm.

"Hah, hah, hah!" a menacing voice snarled. "We have you now, Drew Joyton!"

A girl? A Chiricahua girl who speaks English?

"But which of us gets you first?" This feminine voice was deeper and to his left.

"I want his head," another girl's voice thundered.

I'm surrounded by a pack of Chiricahua girls who all speak English?

He waved the loaf of bread at them and tried to shout. Nothing came out.

"And I say we tie a mule to each leg and draw and quarter him," the first girl suggested.

"We could drown him, Natalie."

Natalie? The Drakeville sisters? It's not Indians?

"Perhaps we should drop him in a rattlesnake den, Nellie."

"Nancy, I think we should hang him by his heels and let the snakes slither down his trouser legs!"

This isn't funny. Why are they saying this? Why can't I talk or move or see them?

Their voices came in an eerie unison: "We have you surrounded, Drew Joyton. There's nothing you can do to get away."

But I can't see you. Where are you?

A girl's hand clamped down on his shoulder. He tried to clear his throat. His voice was no more than a soft whisper. "I . . . can't see anything."

"Neither can I, dear brother. Mama's up, but everyone else in the station is still sleeping. She said I could come out here and check on you. Have you been awake all night, Drew?"

He could smell Blaze's lavender perfume.

"Oh, I dozed a little here and there." *I was dreaming?*

"Yeah, me too. Daddy let the lantern burn down after midnight. Once that happened, I fell asleep. When I woke up, Sarah had her head next to mine," Blaze said.

The shotgun is in my hand. I didn't have a loaf of bread. "I suppose it was a little startling, havin' a milk cow next to you," he whispered.

"Yes. You know how it is right before you wake up. All sorts of bizarre things flit through your mind."

There are no Chiricahuas. "Yeah. Sometimes I have crazy dreams," Drew mumbled.

"Don't tell Mama I said this, but sometimes right before I wake up, I dream of boys. But never boys I know. Just some fantasy boy that my brain makes up. Isn't that strange? Do you ever have dreams like that?" Blaze asked.

And no Drakeville girls! "D-Do I ever dream of boys I don't know?" he stammered.

"No. Do you ever dream of girls?"

I was dreaming! "Yeah, I guess . . . sometimes."

"Are they girls you know or girls you have just seen somewhere?"

Thank You, Lord. I was just dreaming. "Eh, neither. Ah, both."

"Aren't dreams grotesque, Drew? I don't understand them at all."

"Yeah, I, eh, dreamed that I had a loaf of bread in my hand instead of a shotgun."

"It's a good thing you didn't try to take a bite of it. Is Talby up on the roof?"

"I guess so. He talked about doin' something different and then went to get some jerky. I didn't see him after that. Didn't he come back your way?"

"He got some jerky when the lantern was still lit, but that was a long time ago."

"He must be sleepin' on the roof."

"What direction do you think they'll come from, Drew?"

"I've been thinkin' about that. They won't use the roads. They know we'll set defenses there. I was thinkin' they would come up from the south," Drew replied. "That's the way they used to come to this spring."

"But wouldn't they know that we know that?"

"I reckon. What do you mean?"

Blaze's long red hair bounced down to her waist as she sat on the dirt beside him. "Apaches are smart warriors. I doubt if they'd come the way we think they will. Let's say the situation was reversed. Indians were camped here, and you and me were goin' to sneak up on them. How would we do it?"

Drew surveyed the southern mountains. "We wouldn't come up from the north. The mountainside is too steep there."

"And yet . . ." Blaze's voice was almost a song. "If there was a way to climb that north slope, they wouldn't expect us to, would they?"

Drew paused. The sky behind her had faded to charcoal-gray. "There would be no defenses to the north."

"That's where they'll attack, Drew!" she exclaimed.

"Right into the side of the station house with Mama and the ladies!"

Drew scampered out from under the wagon. It was just light enough to make out objects in the yard.

"Come on," he said.

Blaze and Drew sprinted to the low adobe wall that marked the north side of the station yard and the rim of the cliff that dropped down to the floor of the valley.

"Do you see anything?" she asked.

"I can see all the way down, but I don't see anything. Do you see them?"

"Nothing. I don't see anything."

Drew let the shotgun droop to his side. "So they aren't comin' up the slope, are they?"

"Eh, no, I guess not."

"And I left my station," Drew said. "I have to get back to the wagon."

"I'll stay here," Blaze added. "Just in case."

Drew had just reached the wagon when his father hiked toward him.

"You see anything out there, Daddy?"

"Nope . . . it's quiet. No animal sounds. No birds. Not even Talby snorin'. I've got to get some coffee. I'm so tired right now I could lay down in the road and sleep for a week."

Drew hiked alongside his father. They were nearly the same height. "Do you think they decided not to come?"

"They missed their best chance. Did I see you and Blaze over at the station just now?"

"We got to worryin' that maybe they'd pull a surprise and come up that steep north side. So we ran over to check."

"Nothin' there?"

"Nope."

"I'm glad you looked. I checked a couple of times durin' the night even though I don't think anyone could make it up there in the dark. But the cleverest enemy usually attacks at the very point you think impossible."

"Sort of like Satan, I reckon," Drew murmured.

"Now that, son, is a smart thing to figure out for a boy of fourteen." Rand Joyton glanced up at the station roof. "I don't see Talby. Is he up there?"

"I think so. Maybe he's sleeping on the other slope."

"That will be the most important position during daylight hours. Go up there and check on him. We'll need someone alert up there all day. Maybe we'll take shifts."

Drew watched his father duck under the short doorway and enter the stage station. He ran his fingers through his hair. It felt dirty and greasy.

"Hey, Talby, are you awake?" he called out.

He waited. Rhonda and Gertie clucked as they scurried near the hooves of the two milk cows.

"Come on, Tal . . . wake up!"

Blaze appeared from the house. "Is little brother sleeping?"

"I don't blame him. It was a tense night."

"I'm tired, but I did get the cows milked," Blaze said.

Drew climbed the mesquite wood ladder and crept across the thick, faded gray cedar shakes. He paused near the river-rock chimney.

Lord, I forgot what a majestic sight it is up here. I can see the valley below, the pass above us, and twenty miles south. Daddy's right. No one can sneak up on Sonora Pass Station as long as someone is up here.

"Did you find him?" Blaze shouted.

Drew scouted the roof. "He's not up here. Maybe he went to bed inside."

"I suppose he could have snuck in when I dozed," Blaze admitted. "I'll check inside."

Drew surveyed the full horizon, then climbed down. He noticed that the flag hung limp.

Sergeant Thorton ambled toward him. "Quiet night, eh, son?"

"Yes, sir. Maybe we were too cautious."

"Never regret or apologize for your defenses. If you prepared too much, at least you're all safe. And if you didn't prepare enough, well, there's no one left to apologize to."

"Have you seen my brother?" Drew asked.

"Is he missin'?"

"Oh, he's around here. With a station full of folks, we sort of lost our routine."

"Tell your mama we can cook our own breakfast. We don't want you folks to run out of food."

"She'll not take kindly to that. Besides, there's plenty of food at the store." Drew pointed at the big tent.

Blaze hiked out into the yard. "Talby isn't in there."

Drew studied the camp. "I'll check the barn."

"I'll go to the store," Blaze offered.

"The store ain't open yet."

She raised her auburn eyebrows. "I know."

"Hmmm . . . yeah, Kite-Boy just might be there anyway. Hey, did I tell you the Drakeville girls came out to visit with me?"

"In the dark?"

"Yep."

"Which ones?"

"Nancy and Natalie, I think."

"You think? Couldn't you see them?" Blaze questioned.

"Nope. And they both claimed to be Nancy. But the second Nancy said that the first Nancy was really Natalie."

Blaze began to laugh.

"What's so funny?"

"You have girl trouble, dear brother, and you've never even seen the girls."

"It ain't trouble really."

"Sounds like a nightmare to me," Blaze laughed.

"Oh, no, a nightmare is much worse!" Drew sighed as he hiked to the barn.

Rand Joyton pulled a saddle off a big roan mare when Drew entered the adobe barn. "Daddy, have you seen Talby? We can't find him."

Mr. Joyton's white shirt was rolled up to his massive upper arm muscles. "Has Mama seen him?"

"Nope."

"How about the Drakevilles?"

"Blaze is checking."

"I'm sure he didn't wander off too far. Did you ask the sergeant? Talby's probably down visitin' with the teamsters about balsa wood."

"I already asked."

"It's a cinch he won't miss breakfast. I'll be done here in a minute."

Drew meandered back to the flagpole. Blaze motioned him to the front of the store. Mrs. Drakeville stood in a flannel gown behind the open tent flap.

"What did you find out?" he quizzed.

"Mrs. Drakeville said Talby and Nellie visited some last night."

"What about?"

Mrs. Drakeville stood at least a foot shorter than Blaze and Drew. She had folded her arms across her thin chest. "Nellie said that Talby was feelin' bad 'cause you two were heroes, and he didn't do anything but ride in the wagon."

"But none of the male passengers would even do that," Blaze declared.

"He told Nellie he needed to do something heroic."

"What did he mean, heroic?" Drew asked.

Mrs. Drakeville brushed her hair out of her eyes. "He didn't say."

Drew continued to survey the station. "He wouldn't leave camp with Chiricahua Apaches all around."

Blaze slipped her arm into her brother's. "There's nothin' heroic about stayin' in camp."

"You think he went out there?" Drew rubbed his chin.

"No . . . eh . . . yeah . . . he would, wouldn't he?"

"I'll get Daddy!" Drew called out.

"I'll tell Mama," Blaze said.

By the time Drew returned from the barn with his father, most of the folks at Sonora Pass had gathered at the flagpole.

"Sergeant, put men around the perimeter. Looks like the Joytons need to go find little brother," Rand Joyton requested.

"I'll go with you," Possum Summerfield announced. "He came after me and Zink. I couldn't do anything less."

"I'm goin' with you too," Tease blurted out.

"No, you stay here—"

"I need to do this, Mr. Joyton. I really do," Tease begged.

Rand Joyton marched through the crowd. "Okay. The rest of you stay safe. Maybe we won't have to go out of sight of the station. One of you men post a look-out on the roof. We'll start out down to the Flats and then—"

"I think he's up at the pass," Nellie offered.

Mrs. Joyton scurried over to her. "Why, honey?"

"'Cause that's his kite up there!" She pointed high in the pale blue Arizona sky.

"That kid is out there flyin' a kite when he should be—," Mr. Joyton raved.

"What's flashin' up there?" Sergeant Thorton asked.

"He has a mirror hangin' down. I reckon it's catchin' the mornin' light," Drew explained.

"I think it's a signal," Blaze ventured.

"Is that an S-O-S bein' flashed?" Zink asked.

"No . . . no . . . it's O-O-P-S," Sergeant Thorton reported.

"He ran up to the pass, flies a kite, and says oops?" Ceva Joyton fumed.

"No . . . wait." Sergeant Thorton shaded his eyes with his hand. "T-R-O-O-P-S . . . troops!"

"The troops are coming?" one of the lady passengers shouted. "Thank God, we're saved!"

"Shall we go up there and get him, Daddy?" Drew asked.

"Stay on the road where I can see you."

Blaze toted the shotgun and Drew the .45 army pistol as they took the stage road to the top of the pass.

"Did you get my message?" Talby shouted from his rocky perch as they approached.

"About the troops?" Blazed asked.

"Yes. It works. My invention works." Talby climbed down off the granite boulder.

Drew stared up at the bright red kite, drifting high in the air. "It certainly tells the Chiricahuas where you are."

"There aren't any Apaches out here."

"Mama and Daddy aren't real happy about this, Talby," Blaze warned.

Talby's brown bangs hung down in his eyes. "I couldn't just sit around in the dark on the roof."

"When did you hike up here?" Drew asked.

"It was still night. A breeze came up, and I figured I could fly a kite in the dark. And I did. I wonder if that was the first night launch of a kite in Arizona Territory. When daylight broke, it was a beautiful sight to see!"

Drew studied the western slope. "Where are the troops?"

"On the switchbacks near Faraway Perch."

"How many are there?" Drew asked.

"Two."

"Two companies?" Blaze quizzed.

"Or two patrols?" Drew said.

"No. Two soldiers."

"Two men?" Blaze gasped. "That's all that's left of the twenty-nine?"

"There were twenty-nine of them?" Talby asked.

"That's what Sergeant Thorton said," Blaze replied.

"Where's your telescope?" Drew asked. "Is that a stage coming from the west?"

"There are no stages scheduled for today," Blaze told him.

Drew dropped the long brass telescope from his eye. "It's a stage all right, and the way the ponies are runnin', I'd say it's Whap Martin. I'd better get back and tell Daddy."

"I'll stay with Talby and wait for the 'oops' or the stage, whichever gets here first," Blaze offered.

"You goin' to reel that kite in?" Drew questioned.

"I've got it tied off to Needle Rock. I was goin' to leave it."

Drew jogged down the hill to the station. When he got there, most everyone waited for him, guns in hand.

"What is it?" Ceva Joyton called.

"Are the troops comin'?" Sergeant Thorton asked.

"The troops are comin'," Drew puffed. "Two of them."

"What do you mean?" a teamster asked him.

Drew stepped over by the sergeant. "Talby said there were only two soldiers."

"I demand to know where the rest are," the big woman boomed.

"Massacred! That's what it is. The other twenty-seven men were massacred!"

"Daddy, there's also a stage comin' from the east."

"Not today, son."

"I saw it. I think it's Whap Martin."

"Is it a Concord?"

"Yep."

Rand Joyton yanked off his hat. "Maybe it's an express. Must be an emergency."

"If the troops are massacred, what will happen to us?" the big woman wailed. "I think I'm goin' to faint."

"Honey, I'd suggest you go over to the swing and do it," Ceva Joyton advised. "You won't want to be lyin' out here in the road."

The lady stiffened.

The two soldiers on black horses approached the station. Both wore army blue, and one had a lieutenant's stripes. Sergeant Thorton led the surging stage crowd over to them.

"Lieutenant Lindsay, did you run into trouble?" the sergeant asked.

The blond-headed West Point graduate swung down off his horse with seasoned ease. "Just the opposite. The whole renegade band dashed past us and headed to the Mexican border."

"They were swarmin' down toward Sulphur Springs yesterday," Possum Summerfield said. "We got ambushed at Rotten Egg Gulch."

"Thank the Lord, the army chased them out of the desert," the big woman gushed.

"Thank the Lord, but we didn't chase them out. You did," the lieutenant said as he gazed around the station.

"How did we do that?" Drew asked.

"Our scouts captured one of the Chiricahuas before he crossed the border. He said they were goin' north to raid and steal horses, but when the army built a fort at Sonora Pass, they decided to go back to Mexico."

"This is hardly a fort," the big woman blustered.

"Their scouts came up here and saw the big tent and the little ones, discovered the Mexicans making adobe brick down in the valley, and saw the flag raised while a uniformed soldier blew a bugle, and decided there was a whole company of soldiers at Sonora Pass."

"Where are the rest of the troops?" a stage passenger demanded.

"The captain is keepin' them along the border in case the Chiricahuas decide to sneak back in. Meanwhile, we're supposed to go ahead and deliver these logs as planned."

"Do you have time to eat?" Mrs. Joyton asked.

"Yes, ma'am. Be happy to pay for it."

"Oh no, you don't. You have no idea how reassuring it was to see you two ride down that road," Ceva insisted.

The lieutenant tipped his hat. "Thank you, ma'am. But it looks to me like you folks know how to take care of yourselves."

"Here comes the stage," Tease Banyon called out as he trotted toward the road.

Drew turned to see the big Concord racing a cloud of dust to the station. Talby and Blaze rode on top behind Whap Martin and J. J. Jones.

"You want me to help you with a relay team?" Drew asked his father.

"Let's find out what they need first. We won't be timed on an unscheduled stop."

"Ain't seen this many folks since I left Tucson," Whap shouted.

Mrs. Joyton shaded her eyes with her hand. "Do you have any passengers, Mr. Martin?"

The stage door swung open.

"Just him . . . again."

The man in the gray hat stepped down and straightened his suit coat and tie.

"What kind of team do you need, Whap?" Mr. Joyton called out.

"Give me some big boys. I'm racin' right back west. I just came to pick up these folks and get them back on schedule. We promise a twenty-five-day trip from St. Louis to San Francisco, and we'll bust our backs tryin' to fulfill it. Folks, get your belongin's packed up. Me and J. J. is goin' to have some coffee and biscuits with Mrs. Joyton. Then we're headed west."

"Talby," Mr. Joyton called, "you're helpin' me hitch."

"I am?" Talby crawled off the stage. "What about Drew?"

"He doesn't have some serious explainin' to do!"

"I'll help Talby," Drew offered.

"No, you won't," Mr. Joyton snapped.

The stage station came alive with activity. The teamsters hooked up their wagons. Passengers packed. Blaze and Ceva served eggs and potatoes and coffee to everyone who crowded into the dining room.

Drew meandered in and plopped down next to Zink and Possum. "How's your leg, Mr. Chadron?"

"It didn't fall off in the night, and it ain't swollen. So I'm feelin' good. Pain don't kill you, boy. It's gangrene and fever that will do ya in."

Mr. and Mrs. Drakeville burst into the station. "Did you want to see us, Mr. Martin?"

"Got a letter here for you. The stage line has decided they want you to stay right here and build a permanent store."

Ceva Joyton glanced up from serving coffee. "A permanent store up here on the pass?"

"To supply the army camp, I reckon." J. J. grinned.

"What army camp?" the lieutenant asked.

"You see, it's true that stage drivers always get the news first. They're goin' to build a facility called Camp Chiricahua. Since this is the only spring for twenty miles, they want it here."

"An army camp?" Blaze choked.

"Makes sense," the lieutenant commented. "What with the silver discovered down at Sulphur Springs."

"They really did find silver down there?" Drew asked.

The lieutenant scooped steaming eggs up with his fork. "There'll be a rush all right."

"And plenty of need for freightin'," Zink muttered. "We need to get to Tucson and re-outfit."

"Whap, you got room on top for us?" Possum asked.

"You boys is welcome. I'll haul you back for free."

"Did you hear that, Mama?" Blaze exclaimed. "We'll have a town here soon. What do you think about that?"

Ceva Joyton looked out the wide window across the valley to the north and rubbed her narrow shoulders. "I suppose, darlin', it was just too good to last."

NINE

The stagecoach rumbled west up the pass toward Mariposa Junction with seven passengers. Uniformed soldiers led the two big logging wagons in the same direction as soon as the fog from the Concord subsided. Blair Drakeville took his adobe-making Mexican crew back to Cactus Flats to continue their work. Tease Banyon shoveled out the barn after the mules had been corralled. Blaze helped her mother in the kitchen. Nellie hiked up to the top of the pass with Talby to get his kite. Natalie and Nancy were somewhere behind the tent flap and Mrs. Drakeville's apron.

With his thumbs looped in his leather suspenders, Drew stood in the shade of the three cottonwood trees next to the man who held his gray hat in his hand.

"Son, this has been a disastrous trip. First, this man accidentally shoots himself. Then Pinch falls out of the stage. When I got to Tucson, my funds had not arrived. Now I have to return east to check on them. Poor Pinch. I will tell his family about his resting place. I wonder if I should exhume the body and take it back to Santa Fe with me. Is it the one on the left?"

"You can see the marker," Drew pointed out. "It's the one on the right."

"Yes, of course. I don't suppose you have a box I could use for a casket?"

Drew brushed his brown bangs out of his eyes. "We hardly have any lumber up here at all. That's why they're buildin' the store out of adobe. And I imagine the body will be quite dicey by now."

"Yes, but I'll have a difficult time looking at his wife and children and admitting I abandoned the body," the man replied.

"He's got a wife and children?"

"Three little ones."

Drew rocked back on his heels. "We buried him secure, four feet down."

"I'm sure you did, son. Still, if we lived in the East, we would send the body home to the family."

Drew stared at the faded barn-board marker. "What about this other man?"

"I suppose his family needs to be informed too, but I don't even know his name."

"Whap Martin said he got on at El Paso. Maybe someone there knows who he is."

"That could be. If I had them both exhumed, I'd see if someone could identify him."

"I thought you mentioned goin' to Santa Fe. That's the opposite direction from El Paso."

"Of course, but some things are worth a detour."

"It doesn't seem Christian to dig folks up after they've been buried," Drew remarked.

The man stood straight with his hat over his heart. "Nor does it seem very Christian to fail to give their families a chance to bury their loved ones themselves."

"We could send a notice to their families and wait until a family shows up here."

The man studied the hillside. "What family would risk coming way out here?"

"My family, for one."

"Yes, well, according to those passengers, your family has legendary courage. I'm afraid normal families won't be so brave."

"What do you think ought to be done?"

"I'll exhume the bodies if you'll allow me to rent a wagon and team. I'll drive them east for proper interment. Then I'll send the team back as soon as I can."

"I still say the bodies will be rancid."

"I'll do all the diggin' myself, son. I surely wouldn't want you to do something that distasteful."

Drew scratched his dusty, oily hair. "You'll have to talk to Daddy."

"Perhaps you could put in a good word for me." The tall man surveyed the station. "Did I hear that some of those tents are available for rent?"

"I don't know about rent, but they're empty now. Ask Mrs. Drakeville at the store. They belong to her and her husband."

"Thanks. And tell your daddy about my plans."

Drew tramped back to the barn where a girl in a calico bonnet and long dress was talking to Tease Banyon.

"Nellie, have you seen my . . ."

She turned around. Drew's mouth dropped open. *Oh my . . . she's so . . . so . . . so . . . oh my.*

"I'm Nancy."

"Nancy and me was both born in Arkansas. Ain't that somethin'?" Socrates Banyon declared.

"That's n-nice," Drew stammered. "Have you seen Daddy?"

"Now you don't have to mope around," Nancy chided. "I traded you to Natalie for Tease."

"What?"

"I had you. Nellie has Talby. So that left Natalie with Tease, but we traded," Nancy explained.

Tease Banyon shrugged and grinned. "What can I say?"

Why do I get the ones I've never seen? "Where's Daddy?"

"He headed to the station house," Tease said.

Rhonda and her chicks skittered toward the idle swing as Drew ambled to the house. Blaze sat at the bench near the window. A round crochet frame was stretched across her lap.

Drew plopped down. "What're you makin' now, sis?"

"Do you like these yellow and purple pansies?" Blaze asked.

"Sure, you do a nice job. Who're you makin' 'em for?"

"For your wedding present."

Drew leaped to his feet. "My what?"

"Calm down now. Someday, brother, you'll get married. So I'm making these. I'll keep them in my cedar chest until that time."

"But wedding presents? That's a long time away. Besides, you'll get married before me."

"That's probably true. But I have my things all made."

"You do?"

"Certainly. Why do you think I have two cedar chests?"

"Don't get in a hurry." He sat back down beside his sister. "I just saw Nancy Drakeville for the first time, and she jilted me already."

Blaze clapped her hands and laughed. "Oh, I love it. Jilted at first sight. I could write a novel about that. Did she jilt you for Tease?"

"How did you know?"

"He's the only other boy for forty miles."

"You aren't mad, are you? I mean, I thought Tease was chasin' you."

"Oh, no. But I do wonder what she sees in him. I'll have to give that some thought," Blaze said.

"Anyway, I need to talk to Daddy." Drew nodded toward the back rooms. "Is he here?"

"Yes."

"I'm goin' to go see him."

"Please don't," Blaze cautioned. "He didn't sleep a minute last night, and he needs a nap."

"I'll just peek in. If he's asleep, I won't disturb him."

"No, don't do that either."

"Why?"

"Because Mama is in there with him."

"Oh . . . OH," Drew gulped. "If you happen to see Daddy before I do, tell him I need to talk to him about the man with the gray hat."

"What about?"

"He wants to rent a wagon and team."

Blaze flopped her red braid over her shoulder. "Did you tell him no?"

"I told him to ask Daddy." Drew shrugged. "That's not all he wants. It's kind of complicated."

The front door burst open, and Nellie Drakeville marched in. Talby stooped under the low doorway and followed her.

"Hey, what's the guy in the gray hat doin' diggin' in the graveyard?" Talby asked.

Drew tried to peek out the window toward the springs, but the tent store blocked his view. "He's actually diggin'?"

"What's this about?" Blaze asked.

"Eh, he wants to take the bodies back to their families."

"But he doesn't even know that one guy's name," Talby protested.

Blaze strolled across the room. "He's a very persistent fellow."

"I'd better go tell Daddy." Talby headed to the back rooms.

"No . . . leave him alone. He needs to rest," Blaze ordered.

"But this is important. . . . Where's Mama?"

Blaze grinned.

"What's that supposed to mean?"

"It means, Talby dear," Nellie lectured, "that children should go outside and fly a kite."

"Really?"

"That's close enough," Drew added.

"You want to ride down to Cactus Flats with me? I'll show you how to fly a kite from a horse."

"I'll go ask Mama. She might want me to take something to Daddy," Nellie said. They dashed out of the room.

Drew and Blaze peered out the open doorway.

"Did you ever figure Talby for havin' a girlfriend at age twelve?" Drew asked.

"Drakeville girls seem to be quite possessive," Blaze observed.

"Even ones I've never seen. I better go see what the guy with the gray hat is doin'. He's a strange man."

"He has a sneak gun in his boot," Blaze blurted out.

Drew pulled his slouch hat off a peg near the door and shoved it on his head. "How do you know that?"

"I peeked in the window of the stage when I was riding on top. He was adjusting his sneak gun."

"He has a gun in his belt too."

"Why does a man with a gun showing need to have another hidden?" Blaze pondered.

"Perhaps I'll just ask him."

Blaze stepped outside with him. "Be careful, Drew. I'd rather tangle with a rattlesnake or a Chiricahua Apache than a man like that."

"Why is that?" he asked.

"Because as deadly and dangerous as the Indians might be, they are predictable. This man is unpredictable."

Drew passed by the store as he sauntered toward the cottonwoods.

"Hi, sweetie!" The voice filtered out of the tent.

Drew stopped and stared at the dusty white canvas. "Eh, hi, Natalie."

"See, you knew it was me, didn't you?"

"Nellie rode double with Talby down to Cactus Flats, and I heard Nancy in the barn gigglin' with Tease Banyon. So it had to be you."

"My sweetie is so smart."

Drew blushed. "I can't be your sweetie."

"Why?"

"Because I've never seen you face to face."

"Sure you did—last night."

"It was pitch-black. That didn't count, and you were pretendin' to be your sister."

"Why do you have to be so negative, sweetie?"

"I am *not* your sweetie," Drew insisted. Then he hiked toward the springs at the cottonwoods.

The man's charcoal-gray suit coat and black tie were neatly folded and stacked on the wooden headboard leaning against the trunk of the largest tree. His white shirt-sleeves were rolled up to his elbows. "What did your daddy say?"

"Daddy's takin' a nap. You'd better wait until he gets up," Drew advised.

"Fair enough."

"Aren't you goin' to stop diggin'?"

"You buried them about four feet down, right?"

"Yep."

"As long as I'm diggin', I thought I'd dig down about two feet and then stop and wait for your daddy's word. That way, it'll be easy to finish up later."

"I wish you'd wait for Daddy."

The smile dropped off the man's face. "Who owns a grave, boy?"

"Butterfield Stage Lines owns the building over there."

"But who owns these graves?" the man demanded.

"Eh, I don't know."

"Then who is to say whether I can dig here or not? You see what I mean? Normally, it's the family of the deceased that owns a gravesite or maybe a church or a fraternal organization."

"This ain't a regular cemetery," Drew admitted.

"Exactly, boy, and I've spent more time with both of these men than anyone else in this stage stop. Isn't that right?"

"I reckon so."

"Then who's to tell me I shouldn't dig down a couple feet?"

"If you put it that way . . ." Drew peeked down in the hole. "You promise to stop before you get to the bodies?"

"Certainly. You can stay right there and watch me."

"No, I've got chores."

"As soon as I'm down to two feet, I'll be restin' in that last tent. That's the one I rented for the night. I'll talk to your daddy as soon as he's up and around. Does he always sleep in the day?"

"Only when he hasn't slept for three nights. I'll tell him to look you up. Eh, what's your name?"

The man jammed the shovel into the loose dirt. "You know, a lot of folks ask me that."

"They do?"

"Yes, can you believe it?"

Drew rubbed his smooth, round chin. "What do you tell them?"

The man paused and leaned on his shovel. "The same thing I told you."

Drew stiffened. "You didn't tell me anything."

"You're a very smart lad."

Drew hiked to the barn. *Lord, I don't know why that man is so secretive. I always feel strange when I stand next to him. Sort of like with that lady palm reader in St. Louis. It just doesn't feel right, and I don't know why. I'll be glad when he leaves.*

When he reached the open door, he heard Tease laugh and a girl giggle. Drew peered inside.

"Hey, Drew, can we borrow a horse to ride down to the Flats? Nancy wants to see where they dig the adobe," Tease requested.

"Just one horse?"

Nancy grinned. "We'll ride together."

"Eh, sure. Use my horse, Carlos. He's the chestnut gelding. That's my saddle on that barrel."

Drew plodded over to the swing and flopped down in it. He pushed himself until he was swinging out over the north wall of the yard. Then he leaned way back, his head nearing the dirt yard as he swung lower.

Mama's right. This is fun. Just like bein' a hawk divin' for its prey. Zoom!

When he reached the end of the swing, with his feet toward the sky, a smiling woman appeared upside down at the end of the house. Drew stopped the swing, sat up, and turned around. "Hi, Mama! Is Daddy up yet?"

Ceva Joyton's waist-length red hair swirled down her back. "He's sleepin' soundly, darlin'. I think I'll let him rest."

"Your hair looks pretty when it's down, Mama. You ought to wear it that way more often."

"Thank you, Drew Joyton. That's exactly what your father told me. Yours looks like you've been dragging it in the dirt."

Drew jumped out of the swing and brushed his hair with his hand. "Guess I swung a little too low."

"Don't worry about it. Some things are just too much fun to stop. I hear little brother and Miss Nellie went down to Cactus Flats."

"They rode Snickers and took Talby's kite."

"Could you check and see that they made it down safely?" she asked.

Drew glanced at the barn. "You want me to ride to Cactus Flats?"

"No, I was thinking you could go up on the roof to Talby's perch and use his telescope to spy."

"He always takes it with him."

She unfolded her arms and handed the long brass tube to Drew. "He seems to be getting forgetful."

Drew climbed up the ladder and crossed the shake roof to the river-rock chimney. *I think Mama's right, Lord. It'll be real strange havin' people live up here with us. It was nice when Sonora Pass was just the Joyton family.*

The sound of Natalie Drakeville's, "Drew, sweetie," wafted through his mind.

Of course, we have to adapt to whoever You bring our way.

He watched the man with the gray hat saunter back to the little white tent, his dark suit coat draped over his shoulder.

Maybe we don't have to adapt to everyone.

Drew crouched down on the roof and leaned against the rock chimney, resting the brass telescope on his knees. Across the desert floor to the northeast, he spotted a dark cluster of men and animals.

That's the crew making adobe brick. Maybe Talby and Nellie aren't down there yet. Maybe they stopped someplace to . . . Nah, he's only twelve . . . but she's twelve!

Lord, how come girls grow up faster than boys? Talby's tall. He's as tall as Blaze and almost as tall as Mama. But Nellie seems much more mature. I reckon Natalie is more mature than Nellie—a thought which purtnear scares me to death. How come You did that, Lord? You made us bigger and scared of 'em. I reckon that balances out. For a while.

Drew pulled back from the telescope and caught a reflection in the sky.

A red reflection.

The kite! He has the kite flying.

Drew stood up and surveyed the stagecoach road to the west. At Deception Rock, there was dust in the air. The telescope went to his eye.

We've got men ridin' fast.

Maybe six.

No, eight with a packhorse.

No, it's a pack mule.

But why are they in a hurry? Are they bein' chased?

He studied the road behind the men, but could see nothing.

He tramped across the roof to the rustic mesquite wood ladder. "Mama," he called out.

His mother and sister hurried out into the yard.

"Talby's fine. I spotted the kite flying next to the brick-making crew. But we have eight men ridin' hard across Washburn Creek."

"I'll warm up some stew and coffee."

"You want me to help, Mama?" Blaze asked.

"You help Drew with these horses. Let's let Daddy sleep."

Drew and Blaze scurried to the spring with wooden

buckets and filled them with fresh water for the horse trough.

"I see you got the man to stop digging up those bodies," Blaze observed. "But I reckon he'll be back. His coat and tie are over there at the base of the tree."

"He said he'd wait until Daddy woke up."

"I don't want to be around when he pulls them up. That one is dug down to the blanket already." Blaze pointed to the grave on the left.

Drew peered in. "He said he would stop before he got that deep. But I told him they were four feet under. I guess that one wasn't so deep."

They had just filled the trough when a dusty column of men rode into the station.

Blaze shaded her eyes with her hand. "Welcome to Sonora Pass. My brother and I will water your horses if you want to take some dinner inside. Mama has stew and coffee warmin' up."

"Thank you, miss." The lead man tipped his hat. "Is your daddy around?"

"He was up all night and is trying to sleep," Blaze reported. "Is it an emergency?"

The man flipped his vest back, and Drew spotted a badge. "I'm U.S. Marshal E. E. Stillwell. These men are my deputies. We're out of New Mexico on the trail of some men who stole a gold shipment."

"How many robbers?" Drew asked.

"Three men, son. We think they were headed to Tucson. You seen any come through?"

"People come through every day," Blaze told him. "Were they on the stage?"

"I reckon I don't know."

"What do they look like?" Drew asked.

"Washington was about five feet, six inches, medium build with a thick black mustache no wider than his nose," the marshal reported.

"What was his first name?" Blaze asked. "Was it Hadden?"

"No, it was Hamilton. Hamilton Washington."

Drew stared at Blaze. They both glanced at the open graves near the cottonwoods. "I think he's buried over there. There was an H. W. on his suit coat label, but we didn't know his name."

"How did he die?" the marshal asked.

"They said he accidentally shot himself while ridin' in the stage."

"I've been on some stage rides where I wished I was dead," one of the deputies hooted.

"How about the other two men?" Drew asked. "What do they look like?"

The marshal slapped his black hat against his leg and then shoved it back on his head. "Don't have any descriptions, but do have a strange nickname for one of them."

"Pinch?" Drew asked.

The marshal glanced toward the cottonwoods. "You got him buried over there too?"

"Yeah, he fell out of the stagecoach and was dashed to death on the rocks of Diablo Canyon."

The marshal turned his horse back toward his deputies. "This is a deadly route."

"Do you know the third man?" Blaze asked.

"No. No name. Some say he's a hired killer out of New Orleans. Others say he's a dandy, always wears a nobby gray suit."

Drew stepped up close to the marshal and lowered his voice. "He's in the last tent down at that end, but be careful. He has one gun in his belt and another in his boot."

The marshal barked orders. "Two of you men block the road west. Two others go back and block the way east. You two swing over behind the cottonwoods to the south. Son, what's over to the north of the station?"

"A steep incline all the way to the desert floor."

"Can a person ride down it?"

"No, sir. I don't think so. My brother threw a spindle, and it rolled all the way to the bottom."

"Story, you come with me. Let's pay a little visit with Mr. Gray Hat. Don't shoot him unless you have to, boys. We'd like to find that gold shipment if we could. You kids stay behind those trees."

Drew and Blaze trotted to the cottonwoods. Drew stared at the neatly folded gray suit coat. "What is his coat doing here?"

"I suppose he took it off to dig," Blaze said.

"But I saw him hike to the tent with a coat over his shoulder." Drew rubbed the back of his neck. "A dark coat."

"Like the one Mr. Hamilton Washington wore?"

"He stole the dead man's coat!" Drew exclaimed.

He saw the marshal and deputy searching each of the small white tents.

"He's gone," the marshal shouted.

A holler from the barn caused Drew and Blaze to spin around. A rider broke out of the doorway. Tease Banyon ran after the galloping horse.

"It's him!" Blaze called out.

"He's stealin' my horse!" Drew shouted.

The posse galloped toward the rider from three sides. The man with the gray hat spurred the chestnut horse toward the station house yard.

Shots were fired.

Chickens darted every direction.

Drew raced after the man. *He's going to try to take Carlos down the north slope!*

The man in the gray hat spurred the chestnut gelding toward the three-foot-high adobe wall on the north side of the yard.

"Carlos!" Drew screamed. "NO! Whoa, boy! Whoa!"

The big horse tucked his ears back and slid to a stop against the short wall.

The man in the gray hat didn't. He tumbled over the horse's head with a scream that accelerated as he rolled down the steep descent toward the desert floor. Drew ran with the others to the wall and watched him bounce and tumble down the mountain.

Tease whistled. "I don't think I'd like to try that. He slugged me and grabbed the horse."

The marshal holstered his gun and pointed to his tallest deputy. "Story, take three men and ride round to the bottom and work your way up. We'll get some ropes and try to work our way down." He turned to Blaze. "I hope he's alive, miss, 'cause there's a gold shipment to find."

"What kind of crime was it?" Drew asked.

"These three stole a gold shipment to Santa Fe. Hamilton Washington worked as a clerk for the shipping company and thought up the scheme. He and Pinch had been together in the war against Mexico. They spent most of their time in the brig. The man with the gray hat was supposed to be signed on just because of his gun. He was the one that shot the two guards. But the rumor we heard was that he wanted more than his share. The clerk hid the gold and tried to run off, but the other two caught up with him. And that's all I know, except that he didn't have the gold with him. A man with $10,000 worth of gold wouldn't be hangin' around Sonora Pass."

Blaze smirked at Drew. "See, I told you that's what happened."

"Marshal, the man with the gray hat dug up that man's grave to get his coat. He was wearing it when he tumbled down there. So you might check the coat for some clue," Drew declared.

The marshal and deputies had left the yard when a barefoot Rand Joyton scurried out of the station, Ceva at his side. "What did I miss?"

Blaze took his arm. "Come on, Daddy. I'll tell you while you pull on your boots. Mama, it looks like we'll have eight more for supper."

Mr. Joyton glanced around at Drew. "Son, the yard is no place for your horse. I've told you that before."

By noon the next day, the marshal, deputies, and a bruised man with broken legs and a tattered gray hat rode east. Drew filled up the graves and hauled a load of adobe bricks up from Cactus Flats in the afternoon. His white cotton shirt was covered with red dust and sweat when he strolled to the stage station. He stooped to enter the low doorway.

"Wash up. You're just in time for supper," Mrs. Joyton greeted him.

Mr. Joyton studied papers on his desk. "This schedule change is so complex. I can't tell if the westbound express will be here the 6th or the 7th. I suppose I can have a team standing by all day tomorrow."

"Come on and eat," Mrs. Joyton called out. "We know it's not the 6th. That's today."

"No, today is the 5th," Mr. Joyton mumbled. "I don't make mistakes about . . ."

"Well, you did," Ceva insisted.

Rand Joyton studied his calendar. "My word, today is the 6th."

"With all the excitement, it's good that the stage didn't come today," Drew remarked. "Is Tease eating with us?"

"He said he was invited to eat supper with the Drakevilles," Mrs. Joyton reported.

"And Talby?"

"Blaze went to fetch him."

"The Drakevilles' store has become a very popular place for the young men at Sonora Pass," Mr. Joyton observed.

"There is one young man who seems to avoid it," Ceva noted.

"I, eh . . . had work to do, Mama." Drew felt his face turn red.

The door swung open, and Blaze stooped to enter the dining room.

"Where's little brother?" Mrs. Joyton asked.

"He wanted to eat with the Drakevilles," Blaze reported.

Mrs. Joyton stared at the table. "It looks like I cooked way too much food."

"I did bring a guest to eat with us," Blaze announced.

Mr. Joyton and Drew stood as a yellow-haired girl entered the room.

"Mama and Daddy," Blaze announced, "this is Natalie Drakeville." She turned to her brother. "Drew, you know Natalie, don't you?"

Drew felt his legs and arms stiffen. His neck wouldn't move. He couldn't even blink his eyes. His throat felt forged shut. *This is the purdiest girl on the face of the earth. Her face. Her blue eyes. Her lips. Oh, my.*

"Drew?" Blaze pressed.

"Ehh . . . uhh . . . uh."

"Natalie, you sit by the stammerin' young Mr. Joyton," Ceva laughed.

"Are you real, or is this just a dream?" Drew blurted out.

Everyone laughed.

Except Drew.

"Oh, my," Natalie said, "Blaze, I didn't know your brother was such a sweet-talker."

"Neither did I."

"No, I didn't . . . I just—," Drew sputtered. *Lord, help me before I die of embarrassment.*

The door banged open. Talby and Nellie sprinted in. "Daddy, there's a stage headed this way, and it's already at Washburn Creek. I hope they have my balsa wood."

Mr. Joyton jumped to his feet.

"Talby, you fetch Tease. Hold the team comin' in. Mama, you and Blaze set the table for passengers. We'll all eat after they leave. Drew, come on. Let's hitch a six-up relay team."

Drew sprinted to the doorway. *I cried unto the Lord, and He delivered me!*

He had just reached the yard and scurried past Rhonda and her chicks when someone caught hold of his arm.

"I'll come help you, Drew, sweetie," Natalie said.

"Eh . . . do—do you know anything about stage-coaches?" he stammered.

"No, but I'm sure you can teach me," she purred.

For a list of other books
by this author, write:
Stephen Bly
Winchester, Idaho 83555,
or check out his website:
www.blybooks.com